I0589897

Cosmic Decay Debris

COURTNEY HOPE

Also By Courtney Hope:

Secrets of a Party Planner
Cosmic Decay: Contamination
Cosmic Decay: Debris

Coming Soon:

Cosmic Decay: Absolution

Copyright 2019 Courtney Hope
All rights reserved.
Cover Design by Byron Carr

ISBN: 978 0646 808 406

This is a work of fiction. Names, characters, businesses, places, events and incidents are either the product of the author's imagination or used in a fictious manner. Any resemblance to actual persons, living or dead, or actual events is purely coincidental.

Courtney Hope is currently not represented by any publishing organisations. If you wish to represent Courtney, please visit www.courtneyhope.com.au

To Charlotte, Nicole, Sophie and Tabitha

For raising me from the dead and giving me hope again

PROLOGUE

The road can be long and harsh, especially when left abandoned and met with solitude. Deserted cars were left to rust along silent highways, belongings scattered from the trunks, and long-congealed blood smeared on the cracked tarmac.

It had been more than five years since the end of the world. The concrete jungle had crumbled into ruin in a short amount of time and the Earth's population was decimated by a rage-fuelled virus that overtook the collective mind. Humans became the Mindless; scavengers filled with hunger, feasting on bloodlust and hate until it seeped into their bones and devoured them from the inside out. The decay and the rot spread, and all that was left was an empty abyss inside their minds – and outside in their world.

The Mindless roamed listlessly without a fresh supply of anger and blood to fuel their adrenaline. They congregated in cities and towns, stuck in a constant search for food, and when their meals ran out, they wandered and roamed further into the world looking for fresh flesh. But those who were unable to walk - who crawled and clawed their way across the ground - could not leave the places where they'd turned and so they slumped in dormant decay, doomed to be forever hungry.

These Mindless creatures were the product of an otherworldly virus, infected into the population with the intent of destroying it and returning the globe to a natural balance more suited for habitation by those of another world. The Earth was identified as an important and precious resource, and Visitors from this other world wanted to claim it as their own.

With the successful contamination of the human race, the Visitors rejoiced in the world that they were creating. Nature began to reclaim the manmade roads and infrastructures, devouring all in its path. Tree roots cracked the untended roads, and plants began to grow among the rubble. Left in complete freedom, nature took back what had been stolen from it as civilisation had ceased and the planet rejoiced in its renewal.

Animals were beginning to return to the less inhabited areas, though they were still few and far between. They were skittish, distrustful of these new versions of predators who smelled of blood and ripped into the flesh of unwary creatures. The animals of this Earth had learnt to be silent, to exercise their flight reflexes instead of their fight ones, and so they existed primarily unseen in the forests surrounding the decay.

The sun still rose and set with each day, and the seasons still came and went, but they began to return to a pre-climate change environment without man's interference of deforestation and pollution, and relentless advancement.

The Earth itself seemed to rejoice in this rejuvenation, and invited the Visitors in their claim on the jewelled planet. The Visitors had, after all, freed it from destruction.

But others living on the Earth were not so welcoming. Some resourceful humans had survived the contamination and had fought back against the virus, the invasion and then the initial settlement.

Their primitive minds had surprisingly laid the Visitors' plans to waste and caused the first settlers to fail in their duty

3

to cleanse the contamination of Earth. The Visitors had spent years planning and arranging the tools and planting the virus among the human race that inhabited and ruled the planet, and had agreed that the first settlers would systematically remove the contamination – both the virus and any leftover humans. They would then claim the world, signalling to their brethren to join them and continue their dominion of this, their new realm.

The early settlers had not intended that the humans would have survived against their sophisticated and deadly bio-weapons, and had come unprepared for a fight. Distracted by their inflated egos, the Visitors had lost the battle for ownership of the Earth.

But they were determined they would not lose the war.

Across the gulf of space, a fleet of ships filled with Visitors awaited a signal from the first settlers, indicating the success of their mission and the start of a new life on Earth. But the beeping pulse received was actually the signal with a different meaning – a distress signal.

The initial settlement had failed.

The Commander of the Visitors – notable only by the small stripe of neon green light that glowed around the cold metallic cuff it wore on its right wrist – stood at attention behind a control panel. Large oversized metallic panels ran across the bridge and a dark viewing window in front of it opened out to the dark star-filled galaxy.

Positioned around the command room, Visitors usually swarmed around similar controls, moving back and forth on suction-cupped toes. But as the faint beeping reverberated around the metallic command room, they stood stock-still and listened to the last remaining voice of their comrades in arms.

The Commander turned to its fellow guardsmen and let out an ear-piercing shriek that filled the room and shook all from their stupor. They jumped to attention and rushed to their controls as the Commander angrily turned to its own and set a course for the fleet to journey to their new world.

This would not be the entrance they had imaged.

With all of their heavy machinery, weaponry and technological advancements, their superior intelligence and the element of surprise, the Visitors couldn't believe the humans had gotten the better of them and they refused to turn their backs on all they had worked so hard to take.

Their first fleet would not die in vain. This precious world would still be theirs.

CHAPTER 1

Looking for a new home east of their old one, a small group of survivors walked along a lonely and desolate street surrounded by deep forest. The group comprised of four people – a young couple, Max and Victoria Stone, a teenager named Mia Cavallari and a man named Jay Welles.

Max Stone led the group along the road, both hands on a loaded rifle with a black backpack slung over his shoulder. His dark grey cargo pants, light grey shirt and dark cargo jacket were well-worn and he had a fully-stocked bandolier slung over his chiselled shoulder holding his ammunition close at hand. Piercing blue eyes, unkempt shaggy blonde hair, and a five o'clock shadow completed the look of this accidental warrior.

Max was the leader of the small group, and he and his wife Victoria had always been the ones to scavenge supplies necessary for survival. They came up with the plans together and did what needed to be done for the good of the group, but recently Max had been distracted.

He was thinking about Victoria and their unborn child that lay protected inside her womb, unaware of the dangers of the world around it.

Victoria Stone was a determined woman with long brown hair and golden brown eyes. Her dark cargo pants, lace camisole and brown leather jacket covered the slightly rounded bump on her belly, the only indication on her curvy body that she was four months' pregnant. She holstered two pistols in matching gun belts tied around each of her thighs, and circled around her left wrist was a thick metallic cuff.

As Victoria walked behind her husband, she absent-mindedly danced her fingers along her stomach. She sang silently inward to her unborn child and thought about the discovery she had made as she sat in the lounge room of an abandoned apartment, watching to see if something sinister would happen as a result of the invasion by the Visitors from another world.

The Visitors had arrived without warning and with great ceremony, ready to take the Earth from the Mindless that had inhabited it for five years. The small group had taken shelter during the initial Mindless outbreak in a tall apartment building together with Hulio, Diana, Alejandra and Jose Feliz, a Mexican family, as well as Jay's best friend Danny Masterson, a strong-willed African woman named Jacinta Reinhart, and a nervous man named Ian Peters who always looking like he had something to hide.

Curious but wary and determined to survive, the group had been unsure how to react when one of the Visitors came into the building in search of Ian Peters, seeking him out specifically. Ian acknowledged their arrival like a painful repressed memory before revealing to the group that he had been abducted by these Visitors before the end of the world, back when life was monotonous and predictable. In his abduction, Ian had become the immune victim zero in the contamination of the human race and had unwittingly started the Mindless outbreak.

When the Visitor came for Ian, Victoria had attacked the creature and had been mysteriously overcome and taken too. While in captivity and despite being under that numbing spell, she discovered that the Visitors were able to regenerate any amputation or injury sustained on their thick knotted bodies. More importantly though, she discovered the group's chance for survival when she bore witness to the Visitor being attacked by a Mindless on the street and turning into one, only to be killed by another Visitor's metallic wrist cuff.

Victoria was released from the control of the Visitor during the attack and was able to get away, bursting to tell the group that there might be a way they could rid themselves of the Visitors and take back what was left of their world from the Mindless. But on her return, the stubborn Jacinta was determined that her time under the mental control of the Visitor meant she was untrustworthy and needed to be detained away from the group. So for three days she sat in the abandoned lounge room under the watchful eyes of rostered group members, looking outwards to observe the Visitors' next move, and inwardly worrying and planning after discovering the secret that lay locked within her womb – a baby that had only been the size of a rice grain.

Once reunited with the group and her beloved Max, Victoria had informed them of her plan to steal the weaponised cuffs that the Visitors wore and to kill both the Visitors and Mindless, but had not revealed to Max that they were expecting. If her plan had gone wrong then he didn't need to mourn both her and their unborn child. It had been better for him to live on without the extra burden of that knowledge.

If they failed, Max and Victoria wouldn't have wanted to raise a child in a dark world run by creatures from another planet anyway.

So the group had fought. They used the Visitors' weapons against them and in turn sent the Mindless to attack them. When the Visitors were bitten by their own creatures of darkness they were turned and were killed by their metallic cuffs, stolen from them by the survivors. These deaths were final and this knowledge was used against them until there had been nothing left.

Visitors were turned, Mindless were destroyed, and the battle consumed enemies on both sides.

The group had lost many hardened survivors along the way. The entire Feliz family and Danny were all buried in a small park, along with a Mindless named Beth who had been Mia's best friend before the outbreak. Beth had appeared at Mia's old high school while the group were rounding up Mindless to use as a distraction in the battle. It had been devastating to bury their friends, but without Max and Victoria being buried among them, Victoria saw it as the opportunity to celebrate their victory and their life by telling Max the news that they were expecting. Max had been overjoyed, but they still discussed their fears of bringing a child into the world filled with Mindless and the possibility of more Visitors.

The main fear was not their own ability to protect their child, for they now had the hard-fought skills, resources and means to protect themselves from either the Mindless or the Visitors. There was, however, a deep fear rooted in the inability to trust a member of the group who they knew would ruthlessly protect herself above all others.

This person was Jacinta Reinhart, the woman who had distrusted Victoria's intentions so severely that she locked her away from the group for three days.

This action in itself was something that the Stones could forgive, but when Victoria revealed her plan, Jacinta had put her own survival ahead of everyone else's and had refused to fight for the good of their small group, and for the possibility to save mankind.

It had been shocking to everyone to hear of Jacinta's refusal. A world run by mysterious Visitors would mean no chance of a future for humankind, and in fighting a chance existed for them to take back a place on the Earth that could ensure their survival as a species. They were unsure of how many people remained out in the world – alive and at the complete mercy of the Mindless and the Visitors. Even if there had been no others on the planet, it was their duty to ensure that humans didn't face extinction and that the Earth was not completely left to the decay and the destruction of the Mindless and the hostile takeover of the Visitors.

Knowing that Jacinta was not prepared to put others before herself made their already wavering trust in her come to an end. They knew she would give no second thought to killing their crying child if it meant saving herself from a Mindless attack. Their suspicions were proven to be correct when she was entrusted to stay behind at the apartment block they lived in to protect Diana, Alejandra and Jose, who were the least prepared to face the battle. When Jacinta had shown up alone later, casually announcing their deaths, it had confirmed Max and Victoria's fears of her determined self-preservation.

Survival was important, but with no future available would that really be surviving?

So after the battle was won and the dead were buried, Victoria and Max informed the group of her pregnancy and the chance to create a new future for themselves and for the human race – to be the new Adam and Eve as it were. Jacinta had reacted as they expected her to, and so they had argued for her to travel west without the group.

Jacinta had been furious with the decision that was put forward, and argued about how irresponsible bringing a child into the world was. As Victoria and Max stood their ground, Jacinta had no choice but to leave as they all departed from the home they had created in the middle of a warzone. The other lone survivors of the group – the meek and exhausted Mia and the grieving Jay – had been uneasy at the decision, as Jacinta had been forced into helping to save herself and was an excellent fighter against the horde of Mindless that continued to barrel towards them, but seasoned from battle, the group was certainly not helpless and brought their own forms of strengths into play. They chose to travel with Max and Victoria, the leaders who had led them to triumph over the Visitors, and accepted the positive hope for a new world that had started to flicker within them.

Victoria looked up from the thoughts about her and her unborn child and caught the gaze of Mia, walking next to her but several paces away. Victoria smiled at the fifteen year old happily, only to have a tight-lipped smile returned.

Mia Cavallari was not holding up very well in the wake of the Visitor's attack. Her once smooth and childlike face now held tight in a permanent frown, conveying the strain of a heavy burden on her shoulders. She had first appeared to the group two months after the outbreak as a young bookish girl who had escaped alone when her family's farmhouse had been overrun by the Mindless. She had lost everyone she had cared about that day, including her mother, father, her eldest sister Georgia, her middle sister Joan, and Joan's family, including Mia's niece and nephew Rosie and Oscar. But after all of her loss, it had hit the hardest after the battle when she had to bury her best friend Beth.

Mia now wore the weight of battle on her like armour that couldn't be removed. The tears she shed for Beth at her funeral had been her last, and for the past four months she had become more and more hardened and unemotional. She was no longer afraid and would tackle any of the Mindless – no matter how devastating their appearance – without a hint of the terror the meek teenager of the past would have felt.

Even Mia's brilliant blue eyes had hardened, and her look had changed into a cynical adult version of herself. Her long blonde hair was pulled back severely into a ponytail; her black jeans, black tank top and black zip-up sweater reflected her bleak disposition. A black backpack filled with supplies hung off her thin frame and the long silver necklaces she had scavenged glinted in the sunlight.

Victoria had been wary of the new look Mia had chosen when the two of them had broken into a department store for some new clothes that weren't bloodstained, but knew that Mia needed to find herself after her loss. Mia was older then her years now, and her new look matched her hard-edged personality.

The last member in their group, Jay Welles, had also dramatically changed in every way since losing his best friend Danny in the battle against the Visitors. Walking several paces behind them, Jay brought up the rear with his sniper rifle slung onto his back and his pistol tucked into the back of his jeans – but his body rigid, all too aware of the need to spring into action at any given moment.

He was a skinny man who had developed lean, well-defined muscles in the years spent fighting the Mindless, honing his impressive gaming skills into becoming the group's sharpest shooter. He had long black hair that he usually tied into a ponytail, but was now hidden under a grey beanie. He wore a pair of dirty ripped jeans, a ragged black t-shirt and a black leather jacket; the black stubble dotted all over his jaw further authenticating his lack of care for himself.

Losing Danny had forced Jay to grow up from the world that he saw through eyes accustomed to a video game. He had become quieter and more pensive, his dark eyes reflecting a deep hurt. While he was still solid in his presence and determined to protect the small group with everything he had, his easy going manner had toughened and his once-constant joking had ceased.

Victoria felt bad that both Mia and Jay were feeling the loss and decay around them and counted her lucky stars that she and Max were still together, still going strong, and even had something new and exciting to look forward to. It pained her to know that her comrades had lost everything, while she and Max still had each other to hold on to. The group was small and tightly knit, so she could feel the strain when she looked at them.

It felt like one wrong move and the whole group could break apart, shattering like dropped glass.

Victoria didn't begrudge them the looks they threw their way sometimes, or the thoughts she knew were behind their blank emotionless faces. She knew that if anything happened to Max, she would be right there with them, feeling the same knots of pain that they felt.

In fact, she applauded their strengths. If anything were to truly happen to Max, or her newborn baby, she was unsure if she could have kept going, walking on like they did.

They were truly surviving.

The group were making their way to a new home – somewhere protected, with easy access to scavenge supplies and food, and even a possibility to settle in somewhere and start again. They had built a comparatively great life together in the apartment they left four months ago, but it was time to get out of the city and into a new place they could call their own.

They had commandeered a heavy truck from the apartment garage and filled it with all of the supplies that they could carry, and drove through the remains of the city they had lived in, out onto the desolate highway. As they passed the farming area where Mia once lived; she firmly shut her eyes away from the Mindless that wandered aimlessly on the streets near her home.

The truck drove the back roads of the country, passing small towns that set the scene for a dystopian future. Cars were abandoned, rotting bodies lay on the ground, supplies scavenged. Moving away from cities and sticking to back roads was their best option as they left their past further behind them.

Eventually, the truck they had been using ran out of gas. They had walked to nearby villages and towns looking for a gas station or an abandoned car they could siphon, but none eventuated. All cars had been sucked dry, perhaps by other survivors, or the gas had simply evaporated into the air under the heat of the sun. Whatever was available they collected, but what they could scavenge was becoming scarce. They faced the frightening realisation that they had to continue their journey to find their new home on foot – or at least until they found a workable vehicle.

And so they walked. And walked. And walked some more.

They sought shelter where they could, and found sanctuary in small places – an abandoned cabin made of thick timber logs where dust had collected on the threadbare rugs; a small camp they erected from canvas tents scavenged from a country camping store; even in the middle of the road, where they slept on hard concrete, and in paddocks with backs leaning against prickly trees. But no matter where they set themselves up they were never alone; the Mindless stumbled upon them, attacking them mercilessly when their guard was down.

Their outlook was as bleak as the grey weather and the destroyed landscape around them.

But still Victoria had hope. There had to be something left, some little corner that they could call their own, where they could set up a home and raise their child. This quest for a refuge was why they found themselves on this desolate road surrounded by forest, hundreds of kilometres away from their pre-apocalypse home. They were all getting weary, but their search for sanctuary kept them putting one foot in front of the other.

It was Max who spotted it first; one of the Mindless wondering aimlessly on the road, making soft shuffling sounds.

It was a woman with long tangled brown hair covered in mud, wearing an oversized dress and faded wool jumper, now splattered with blood and dirt. She spotted the small group and turned to face them, shuffling faster as she began to pick up surprising speed – the Visitor's contagion beginning to pulse in her veins as she started towards them.

Max slung his rifle over his back and pulled a hunting knife from a sheath strapped to the belt of his pants. He broke into an easy jog, calculated his aim, and met the Mindless at the side of the road, driving his knife deep into her skull. The Mindless woman let out a squelching groan before falling, in final stillness on the road.

Max started to wipe his knife on his cargo pants when he stopped suddenly, standing over the body on the road. He was staring intently at something in front of him.

Heightened by his sudden stillness, the group stopped in their tracks.

"Max, what is it?" Victoria asked, feeling her body beginning to tingle with a more human adrenaline – the fight or flight nature of humanity beginning to kick into action inside of her.

"I think we may have found something good," Max called from his position just up the road. He waved the group forward and they walked quickly towards him. Jay jogged to catch up as he had been walking somewhat behind the women.

They all reached the side of the road to where Max was standing and he pointed to a metal sign on two steel poles on the side of the road.

The sign read *Mt. Beryl Marina, Next Exit.*

"What do we think of checking out the marina?" Max asked. "It'll be surrounded by water on one side so it could at least be somewhat protected, and if there are any boats they could have fuel and supplies."

"Anywhere is better than spending another night on the road," Mia said, her voice sounding thin and bored.

"Let's do it," Victoria said in agreement, trying to ignore Mia's lack of enthusiasm. Jay nodded next to her. Max pointed out the next exit a few kilometres up the road and they all took off together, walking with a quickened pace. They didn't have too much longer until the afternoon sunlight would begin poking its head through the trees, and they were keen to get settled and safe before nightfall.

The small group reached the bend in the road quickly and walked down the exit that promised the Mt. Beryl Marina. The exit road was rockier than the highway had been and the road narrowed to become smaller and more secluded, surrounded by thick trees and forest that encroached on the broken tarmac. Despite the harder going, Victoria gave a sigh of relief to be off the main road and away from the dangers that a highway could bring.

After another ten minutes of solid walking, worrying slightly that they had mistaken the sign on the highway, the forest around the road began to clear and they came across a sign for the marina built into a low sandstone brick wall. Behind the wall was an expanse of overgrown green lawn dotted with imported palm trees giving the marina's grounds the feeling of being on a tropical island. Discarded and dropped palm fronds lay sinking into the overgrown grass and the rocky path snaked its way into a large parking lot that was marked with some seemingly randomly placed sandstone boulders.

A few expensive looking cars sat abandoned and rusting in the large parking lot of the once manicured grounds, but they guessed the majority had been stolen or used to flee in when the world began its sharp descent into chaos all those years ago.

Beyond the parking lot was a large grey painted building that looked like it used to house boating facilities, a function room and a restaurant. It sat in front of a large embankment and beach and two long piers made of dark, rotting wood that led to a few abandoned yachts and dinghy's that were anchored to the pier. One of the smaller boats had overturned completely and bobbed uselessly in the water.

A collection of decaying bodies and body parts lay on the beach, probably washed in from the ocean during a large storm that had halted the groups' travel only a few nights before. Some of the severed arms and hands twitched uselessly, still connected by ligaments to the heads and chests of the Mindless who were still animated but half-eaten by fish and battered by the unforgiving sea.

A Mindless wandered around the marina's restaurant balcony restlessly. When it saw the group of four standing at the edge of the car park it made a loud groaning sound and outstretched its arm towards them. It moved forward vigorously, reaching for them, and managed to topple itself over the balcony's glass railings, landing with a wet splat on the ground. Victoria turned her head away from it, feeling her morning sickness threatening to rise.

She had no idea why they called it morning sickness when it happened at any point during the day. Victoria had managed to keep the nausea at bay most of the time, but she had found that it had made her a little more squeamish when it came to the permanent and usually messy demise of the Mindless.

Groans rode the wind from the direction of the beach and the pier, but they were muffled indicating they were trapped in their watery prisons. Max signalled a quick command to Jay and Mia before they took off towards the building entrance to dispose of any Mindless who lay inside. Victoria and Max walked towards the beach, its water filthy as it lapped around them, mixing seaweed with human remains. Max began the quick process of driving his hunting knife into the skull of any of the Mindless who lay twitching on the beach.

The morning sickness continued to rise inside her and Victoria chastised herself for feeling so weak and sick as her husband took it upon himself to rid the area of the Mindless and make it completely safe for them. She struggled to hold onto the contents of her stomach when she could hear the soft dying groans of a Mindless nearby and closed her eyes tightly, focusing on the lazy rolling sound of the ocean and imagining the gentle lapping of the waves on the beach.

Suddenly, the waves in her mind began to shift and become a bright white, blazing so brightly in her mind's eyes that if she had been looking directly at the colour she would have burnt her retinas. Her very mind was illuminated with hot white light that began to flash at the edges and she felt disconnected from her body, like it was not her own. Her only feeling came from a searing pain in her womb that began to reverberate through her very blood, coursing throughout her body.

Victoria had felt this pain before – when she had been spellbound by one of the Visitors from another planet as she had attempted to rescue Ian Peters. The Visitor had enslaved her in the burning pure light, and she had been powerless to do anything other than its voiceless bidding. When it had been attacked by the Mindless as it brought them back to its ship, Victoria too had felt the searing agony the Visitor had felt as the Mindless clawed into it. The pain and the light had dissipated with the Visitor's loss of control, and Victoria hadn't felt it since. Why was she feeling it now when the Visitor's had all been destroyed?

Victoria suddenly felt terrified.

With everything she had, Victoria retreated into herself and forced a calm over the pain, blocking out every sound, light and sensation around her but the waves on the shore. All she could feel was the cool sea breeze and all she could hear were the waves washing over the sand. . Slowly her vision began to clear from the brilliant haze. Her body rigid with tension began to relax and her connection to the world around her began to return. Victoria could only just make out the muffled tones of Max as he spoke to her while he walked up and down the short expanse of beach near the marina.

"I think this is going to be the best that we're going to find for now," Max told her in a thick voice that was being carried away with the breeze. "We don't have much longer to keep looking and we need to start hunkering down for the night and prepare. I don't think we're going to find a more secure spot than this."

Victoria breathed in and out to the sound of the waves, her eyes still closed and her head down, hands resting on her knees as the nausea and the searing bright lights finally subsided.

Suddenly, a gunshot rang out across the quiet expanse of the beach, pulling Victoria violently from her meditation and causing her to spring upwards at the ready. Max was a little way away from her on the beach, and together they looked out towards the pier where the gunshot had come from.

Jay was standing on the rotten wood of the pier with his right arm outstretched in front of him; his pistol a smoking extension of himself. A Mindless had been walking towards him on the pier and he had fired his pistol straight into it. The Mindless had fallen backwards onto the deck as the bullet tore through its decaying skull. Jay walked silently over to it before putting his black steel tipped boot to its shoulder and rolling it over the marina's pier and into the cool water below.

"Jay!" Max called from his place on the beach, "No more bullets OK? We don't want to draw any unnecessary attention to this place!" Max waved at his friend, who looked over his shoulder in their direction. Jay suddenly went rigid and quickly drew his pistol up again, aiming it directly at them, ready to fire.

"Too late," said a deep voice from behind. Surprised at hearing a strange voice so close behind her, Victoria whipped her head around, and found herself staring straight down the barrel of a gun.

CHAPTER 2

Victoria let out a surprised gasp as her eyes widened. The barrel of the gun was aimed directly at her forehead, right between her eyes and its cold muzzle was all she could see. Her mind raced, struggling to comprehend the situation and work through possible scenarios.

Victoria thought of acting quickly, swiping the pistol from in front of her face, but in her mind she saw the gun fire and lodge a bullet in her leg, or in Max, or misfire and hit Jay standing across the beach behind them at the pier. Her mind played out the man reacting and attacking, fighting her until he had her in his well-muscled arms facing her husband with the pistol, once again aimed directly into her temple. Victoria saw Max rush in and be shot by another assailant standing behind the man that was threatening her. She saw Jay firing his aimed pistol from across the beach, killing the man before his group then reacted and killed everyone else.

So many bad endings raced through her mind in that split second where time seemed to stand still.

As her mind contemplated ways that they could all get out of the situation with minimal damage, Victoria then thought of the baby inside her, curled up and tiny, needing protection … and needing her alive.

Victoria knew that if she reacted impulsively, her child would not get out of this alive, and Victoria needed it alive. She needed this baby – the world needed this baby if it was ever going to be like it was before.

Victoria raised her forearms in surrender and dragged her mind back to the present. She took in the threat beyond the gun barrel that she was looking down. The man with his pistol aimed at her face was muscly and strong. He had slick, dark skin, a shaved head and a face clear of beard or even a five o'clock shadow, meaning that he and his group were holed up somewhere safe with plumbing and supplies. He wore camouflage pants and a grey cotton tank top with a rifle slung over his back. She saw the brief shine of a chain with dog tags attached that hung around his neck and guessed him to be military, or ex-military now that the official government-sanctioned military didn't exist anymore.

Victoria breathed heavily, glad that she hadn't followed her first instinct of attacking him. He would have taken control of the situation easily.

With him, and just a few steps behind with guns raised and aimed at Max and Jay, was an Asian man and a beautiful dark-haired woman. The young man was slim yet strong, though not as muscular as the dark-skinned man. He wore a faded and dusty blue denim shirt with the sleeves rolled up to the elbow and a pair of dusty cargo pants tucked into well-worn brown boots. He had a secure backpack buckled across his chest with the handle of what looked like a sword sticking out of it. He had his gun pointed directly at Max.

The woman had her shotgun raised and pointing to just beyond Victoria's shoulder at Jay. She looked vaguely familiar to Victoria, and had thick raven coloured hair that was slightly dishevelled but clean, unlike Victoria's brunette braid. She knew given the situation it was ridiculous, but Victoria instantly felt unattractive next to this naturally gorgeous woman, who had pale porcelain skin and brilliant blue eyes. She was very thin and stood with excellent posture and purpose – strong and direct.

"It seems you have come across what we might call a goldmine here," said military man holding the gun to Victoria's forehead. "Thanks so much for clearing it out for us."

"Please," Max said, still standing on the beach away from his wife, his hands also raised in the air. "Please, don't shoot my wife. You can have the marina, but just please let us go."

"How many are there of you?" the man asked Max, turning slightly in his direction. "Are we missing anyone else here besides you three?"

"You're missing me!" the sweet voice of Mia was carried across the sea breeze from the balcony where the Mindless had fallen from only a few minutes before. Suddenly a shot rang out and landed at the military man's foot, causing everyone to jump.

Victoria jumped in place, squeezing her eyes shut and praying that it wasn't the end. Max jumped towards Victoria, looking to save her from a bullet, while the military man jumped back slightly from the bullet hole that sizzled where he had been standing.

As fast as they had moved, the Asian man re-aimed and cocked his gun at Max, who stopped mid-jump a little closer to Victoria and slowly raised his hands again. The woman aimed her gun into the direction of the shot but struggled to locate Mia, who had disappeared into the building. The military man stepped forward again and put his gun barrel directly onto the middle of Victoria's forehead.

She could feel the cold metal kiss her just above the bridge of her nose, the skin on her forehead wrinkled slightly from her squeezing her eyes tightly shut.

"Try that again and I blow her head off," the man boomed into the air. "I take it you wouldn't want that to happen, so why don't you all come down here and re-join your friends ... slowly. You too tough guy," he nodded his head in Jay's direction across the pier, who still had his gun raised.

Victoria slowly unwrinkled her forehead and opened her eyes. The gun barrel and hand holding it were blurred and disjointed being so close in her vision, and the whole thing seemed surreal. She looked from the barrel of the gun into the chocolate brown eyes of the man holding her at bay and fumed silently at him. He must have felt the hatred radiating from her steely gaze because Victoria saw one dark eyebrow jump slightly and his eyes flickered.

His eyes held no mark of the red iris that was common in the Mindless but for some reason Victoria couldn't help but recall the flicker of Ian's eyes back at the apartment when the Visitors had first arrived on Earth. Ian had looked at her in terror and she had seen human eyes reflected back at her with the red iris of the Mindless, but also a ring of electric blue. She had come to see that electric blue as the mark of the Visitors, but she was always surprised at the intensity that eyes could evoke.

Victoria heard a crunching sound to her right that pulled her from the staring contest with her captor. Her eyes flicked over to the sound to see Mia and Jay approaching slowly. Their guns were drawn and pointed at the intruders in the same way that they were pointed at them. Victoria, Max, Jay and Mia outnumbered the group for sure, but if someone started shooting there would be no way that everyone would be able to get out alive.

"That's all of us, I swear," Max piped up from his position to her left. "Please, lower your gun on my wife. We won't attack you, we promise. You can just let us go and we can be on our way."

Victoria saw Mia seethe from where she stood with her gun raised at the beautiful woman, unwilling to promise to let them go. The man holding the gun to Victoria's head took a step backwards so that the barrel was no longer pressed against her head and the whole group shifted uncomfortably.

"Please," Max tried again. "Lower your weapons and we will lower ours." He shot a look at Jay and Mia standing to Victoria's right, who after what seemed like forever, both lowered their weapons from being levelled at the heads of the woman and the Asian man.

The reaction for the woman and the man was hesitant, but they too lowered their weapons from the group. The military man with the gun to Victoria's head was slower to end his hostage situation.

"Please. Can we talk?" Max asked him, stepping backwards again.

"Wife, huh?" The military man finally spoke after a moment. "That's rare nowadays. I take it you're the leader then?" he asked Max directly, who nodded slowly. "Where are you from?"

"We've been on the road for about four months," Max answered. "We were holed up in a city quite a distance from here, but when the …" He stopped himself before mentioning the Visitors, unsure of how that would be taken. Did this group know about their arrival? It had been so far away from where they stood that it seemed unlikely. "We had to leave. We've been looking for somewhere safe ever since. My wife is pregnant."

The militant arched one dark eyebrow and looked at Victoria's soft belly in a judgemental fashion. Victoria slowly lowered her arms to cover her stomach in a protective movement.

"That's an unfortunate situation," the man finally said, breaking eye contact with Victoria's body. "We have someone who might be able to help take care of that."

Victoria felt anger suddenly bristle like imaginary heckles on her body, and she narrowed her eyes at the man.

"We want this baby. We don't want someone who might be able to 'take care of it' for us," she told him angrily. "This world needs to live on somehow, and how else do you expect that to happen? You don't know anything about us. You don't know what we've done to make sure our world is able to keep going. You should be thanking us for what we have done."

The militant arched his eyebrow again. "And what exactly have you done?"

Victoria stopped short. Like Max had been thinking when he had stopped short of explaining it, Victoria knew that the battle they had waged against the Visitors from another world seemed incredible. She also knew that if she hadn't been there to witness it – to see the Visitors arrive with her own eyes – then she wouldn't have believed it herself. Victoria knew that this group of strangers would find their tale hard to believe, and wouldn't consider letting them go. They would seem crazy; a liability. They would be killed for it.

The man continued to stare at Victoria, unwilling to let the question go. She had to say something.

"You wouldn't believe us even if we told you," Victoria told him quietly.

"So it's like that is it?" the man asked. "You've done something so miraculous that you deserve to live, but you won't tell us what? You know how much that is worth to us? Nothing." The man called it like it was and Victoria wanted desperately to scream at him, to tell him of the Visitors and the war. But she knew telling this group wouldn't help the situation change. They were at their mercy and that was all there was in this world.

One mercy after another until there wasn't anything left.

"What are your names?" asked the beautiful woman, speaking for the first time. Her voice was clear and her pronunciation was concise. She sounded pleasant to listen to and still somehow familiar to Victoria. Her voice wasn't as hard as the military man and it raised Victoria's hope in the situation a little.

"What does it matter what our names are?" Mia spat at the lady in a harsh tone that made Victoria wince. Mia's seething anger was making the situation worse.

"If everything else you have is worthless, you're names just might be worth something to us," the dark skinned man replied, turning his gaze in Mia's direction and meeting the scowl on her young face.

"We're looking for someone in particular. If you have any information that would help, it could buy your way out of this." The woman instructed Mia in particular but spoke to everyone, also trying to dissolve the rising tensions between the groups.

"Whoever you are looking for they don't exist anymore," Mia said curtly, but it was the final slap in the face. The militant man cocked his gun once more and this time raised it directly at Mia's head.

"Woah, woah, woah!" coaxed Max, his hands rising in the air once more. "It's OK! We are happy to help in any way; we just don't have to resort to that! Look, my name is Max Stone and this is my wife Victoria. That's Jay Welles over there and she's ..."

"Don't," Mia cut him off, staring intently down the barrel of the gun. "They don't get my name."

The military man's dark brown eyes pierced right into Mia's as he stood tall and hard against the gun barrel.

"Don't make the biggest mistake of your life girl," he told her softly. "What is your name? That's all we want to know."

"For crying out loud Mia!" Victoria yelled at her friend, finally breaking the spell of rage and confidence the fifteen year old girl was wearing like armour. Her eyes darted in Victoria's direction and she could see the anger flash through them like a wildfire.

Mia may have had a death wish since losing Beth and her family, but Victoria was in no way going to let her endanger herself and the group on her watch.

The Asian man and the beautiful woman shifted suddenly and looked at each other, while the military man continued to hold his gun to Mia's head, unmoving.

"Mia, huh?" the beautiful woman asked kindly, "What's your last name Mia?"

"Why do you care?" Mia asked the woman.

"Why do you have such a death wish?" she answered. "Things don't have to be so hard in this world you know?"

Mia's eyes darted once again over to Victoria who shot her a pleading look. This had gone on long enough.

"Cavallari," Mia said through gritted teeth. She moved her eyes back over to the woman and stared her down. "It's Cavallari, OK? Are you happy now?"

The woman suddenly broke into a mega-watt smile that seemed to light up the beach, taking Mia by surprise. The military man instantly dropped his gun back down to his side and stepped away from Mia.

"I am actually. You all just bought a one way ticket to come with us," she replied with the huge smile still on her face.

"Please, you have our names. Just let us go and we can keep walking. We don't want any trouble," Max tried to bargain with the group.

The militant shook his head and smiled as well, showing a line of straight white teeth that seemed to gleam against his dark lips. Victoria strangely looked at the smiles that were now being thrown around and found herself longing for a toothbrush and some toothpaste.

"I'm afraid you're going to have to come with us," he answered. "Grab your stuff and let's start walking." He brandished his gun in the direction of the road that they had come from and raised his eyebrows again.

The group hesitated, but then Victoria and Max gathered their belongings, preparing to go back the way they came. As they picked everything up, the two men and the woman made for their various weapons and took them. The military man and the woman stowed Victoria and Jay's pistols in the back waistband of their jeans and the young man swung Max and Mia's rifles over his broad shoulders, despite Mia's glare that she shot in his direction.

They started walking in formation up the long driveway from the marina with the woman leading the way and the two men taking up the rear, their guns drawn and ready should the group surprise them.

Mia edged closer to Victoria and whispered in her ear; "When I tell you not to give out my personal information, you need to listen me," she told her harshly.

"When our lives are at stake, I'm going to do whatever I need to do to make sure that we all get out of there alive," Victoria answered just as sternly.

"I can take care of myself Victoria," Mia fumed at her, "You're not my mother."

Victoria felt stung by Mia's words. She knew well and good that Mia was not her daughter, but she had come to love her as if she was.

"I know I'm not Mia. But that doesn't change the fact that I am your friend and I still care about you," Victoria told her. "I know you're hurting right now and I want to help you if you just let me in, but all of this is bigger than you and your death wish."

"Oh right, it's all about you and your unborn child isn't it?" Mia spat angrily, taking Victoria by surprise with so much resentment in her voice. Victoria already felt guilty that the group had gone through so much and had lost so many people close to them yet Victoria still had Max and now had a child on the way.

But she had lost other people she had cared about too. She'd cared about Diana, Hulio, Alejandra, Jose, Danny, Ian and yes, even Jacinta. Victoria was stung, because she only wanted to do what was best for all of them; for humanity.

"You know what Mia? It *is* about my unborn child and me. But it's also about you, and Max and Jay," Victoria told her, trying not to let her voice waver from the hurt that she felt. "How would you have felt if they had shot Jay instead? It may not seem like it to you right now, but we all want the same thing. After everything we've done, and everything we've been through, we didn't survive the plague of the Mindless and we didn't survive fighting against the Visitors for it to end right now in the hands of humans with a gun."

Mia fumed silently at this, her eyes screwed up in rage.

"Not all of us survived," she answered, her voice softening slightly and Victoria knew she was lost in her thoughts of lost loved ones.

"But you did," Victoria told her, trying to clip the edge from her voice to match Mia's. "You did, and we did. Doesn't that count for something? Doesn't that prove that there is still something to live for, something to keep fighting for? I know you want to give up, but you're not done yet. And I'm not going to let you."

Mia hung her head and dropped her scowl, her face smoothing into a worried expression. Victoria knew she had gotten through to her, but knew that this wasn't the time and place to continue to have a deep conversation. Just because they had avoided being shot at the beach didn't mean they would make it through the night back at this new group's camp. She had no idea what to expect from the coming meeting, but Victoria knew they all had to be on the same page.

The group walked for what felt like an hour. They had double backed to the highway and had continued walking back the way they had originally come in the direction of the city they had once lived in. The two men and the woman must have been following them for quite some time and Victoria fumed that they hadn't realised.

The woman directed the group into the forest and they all walked among the pine trees, stepping over roots and beds of dried leaves. Max, Jay, Victoria and Mia walked as quietly as possible through the forest but the woman and the two behind them didn't bother in quieting their footsteps. Victoria found it odd that three people who had been quietly following them this whole time were being very loud in their tracks until they stalked past a pile of clearly charred bodies half covered with fallen leaves. She looked at the woman who didn't even bother to look down at the pile and Victoria realised that they had cleared this section of the forest so they must be closing in on their home base.

The group continued to walk uphill until they reached the summit and came out into a clearing. At the forest perimeter was a makeshift fence made out of trees that had sharpened sticks and trunks sticking out at odd angles.

Victoria saw a Mindless woman caught on a large stick that protruded from the fence, impaled through her middle and unable to escape. She was relatively young and small under all the dirt and decay, and she had fallen leaves and pine needles sticking out of her dull brown hair. She wore a long flowing blush pink dressed that was covered in dirt and dried blood, especially at the knees.

A large stocky man with slicked-back black hair was standing on the inside of the fence next to her. When he saw the group approaching, he stuck a dagger straight into the eye of the Mindless and pulled it out again, ensuring that the Mindless woman stopped struggling and humped forward under her own frail weight. The man wiped his dagger on the woman's bony shoulder and then sheathed it in its holder under his black leather jacket before starting in their direction.

"What do we have here?" the man asked as he approached, his voice thick with an accent that Victoria couldn't quite catch.

"You should get her," the beautiful woman told him from outside the fence as she waited for him to flip a latch and open the gate that they stood at. "She's going to want to see this."

As the group walked through the gate and into the compound, Victoria stole a look around. There was a large brick house in the centre of the clearing where they now stood that looked almost like a manor. The house was somewhat dilapidated with strands of ivy growing up the sides of the walls which were patched with cement here and there, but it seemed comfortable and had a distinct flavour of old money about it – back when there was money.

A veranda snaked its way around the right side of the house and piles of wood were stacked against the brick walls on the left, ready for a fireplace. Victoria noted that the wood pile had the base of a tree trunk rooted near it with an axe wedged deep into the base, ready for splitting.

She quickly calculated how long it would take to run to the axe and recognised that with the military man and this thick-accented stocky man as well, Victoria was sure she wouldn't get very far. She sighed inwardly, and turned her attention back to the house.

A woman was walking out of the sturdy wooden door and down the veranda steps. She had chestnut brown hair that was a little longer than her shoulders and her eyes were a bright blue colour that Victoria was certain she had seen before. The woman was a slim build, dressed in jeans and a brown elbow-length shirt and her face had a very familiar structure to it.

Suddenly, Victoria realised where she had seen this woman before, and realised what all of this was about.

"Mia?" the woman called, hesitating like she couldn't believe her eyes, stopping in her tracks.

Mia, who had been looking around the clearing and had been focusing on the axe in the same calculating way that Victoria had just been, turned her head sideways and took in the woman. Her similar blue eyes widened in shock.

"Mia!" the woman cried again and started running towards her. Mia stumbled slightly as she reached out to her clumsily in return.

"Georgia?" she asked, naming her eldest sister in disbelief.

Georgia raced to her and grabbed her by the shoulders, throwing her into a hug, Mia was standing stock still as Georgia enveloped her, hardly believing this could be real. Suddenly, everything melted away, and Mia wrapped her arms around her sister's familiar frame in return, holding so tight she looked like she would never be able to let go.

Everything unlocked inside of them and for the first time in four months, Mia gave way to her emotions and sobbed. After being so distanced from everything around her, Victoria could see that Mia finally felt at home.

CHAPTER 3

"What happened to you?" Mia asked, pulling away from the hug but still holding onto Georgia. She was unable to fully let go of her sister that she had long believed was dead. Mia took in her sister's face and saw the same familiar features she saw in herself. Georgia was slightly thinner and her face wore a look that was weary and tired, but she was still as beautiful as Mia had remembered.

When she was younger, Mia had idolised Georgia. She had always seemed so wild and carefree, daring to adventure out into the world in a way that was the complete opposite of the country lifestyle they had led with their parents, their other sister Joan falling in behind them. Mia wanted nothing more than to follow Georgia's footsteps into the city and always looked up to her for being brave enough to live the life she had always wanted.

Even if she had left Mia behind.

After the first outbreak in the city that fateful day, Georgia had high-tailed it out of her city apartment and made her way back to her family at their country farmhouse at the edge of town. Mia's father, and Georgia's namesake, George Cavallari, was a veterinarian who specialised in horses and livestock in the rural area surrounding the town, and had been determined to stay at the family farm even as groups of the Mindless wandered up the road along the highway. They had lived there for practically their whole life, and he wasn't prepared to leave everything behind despite Georgia trying to convince him to do so.

Mia's family hadn't witnessed the outbreak in the town, and she had been thankful for that. Her mother, June, was a modest fifties-style housewife who was set in her ways and too kind in her heart to witness such horror. The same went for middle sister Joan, who took on their mother's nature like a second skin when she married her dim-witted but kind-hearted husband August Burns. They had two children named Rosie and Oscar and had all lived together in the farm house with Mia and their parents.

It had been a lot of family for the teenage Mia to have around.

They had all been too timid and scared to leave the farmhouse after Mia came bursting in that day after school screaming about an attack that had happened on the bus. It had been a hard tale to believe, but the nightly news on the television had confirmed the rioting Mindless. The reports continued until all the stations went down a day later. In the end, only Mia and Georgia had actually seen the Mindless in their rotting flesh.

Until the fateful day came that ripped their family apart.

It had been almost three months after the initial outbreak. Outside communications had ceased completely, but hope they would somehow avoid all the horror had never strayed far from their minds – simplicity was in the Cavallari's nature after all.

But on that fateful day, a hungry horde had started their departure from the concrete jungle, searching in vain for a food supply that had run out in the city. Eventually, the Mindless stumbled upon the farm. They had attacked August first, who had been in the forest nearby hunting fresh meat for the family. He had started running back to the house, screaming, but he had always been a portly man and never had a chance to outrun the rampaging horde

Mia had been standing on the back porch with Joan and Georgia, yelling at August to hurry, when they saw him taken down. Joan let out an ear-splitting scream that alerted the Mindless to the farmhouse itself, and Georgia and Mia had tried to pull her inside as she kept screaming and reaching for her husband as he was devoured in the fields.

Georgia had eventually been able to drag her sister in; Joan was absolutely hysterical. Georgia had pulled her into the laundry that was just inside the back doorway and she pulled her around to face her. Georgia slapped her hard across the cheek to get her to stop screaming. Joan fell silent for a moment as Georgia told her to be quiet, but a commotion heard in the entrance way at the front of the house pulled the girls away from each other.

Joan started hyperventilating, raking her fingers across her face in sheer terror, but Georgia left her by the back door and ran through the cold tiled kitchen towards the farm house's front entrance. Mia had followed Georgia – always the strong one of the sisters – and raced through the kitchen where her father had been preparing the evening meal. Mia had rounded the corner of the kitchen doorway to find three Mindless had broken through their front door.

They had been two men and a woman when they once were human. The woman had bedraggled looking dirty blonde hair and was wearing a tattered dress and sweater. The men were dressed in an assortment of ragged clothes; one of them in a ripped suit jacket and dangling tie with his jawbone ripped out from under his face, the other with dark matted brown hair was wearing casual clothes that showed off three large gaping and clotted bite marks in his thighs. All of the Mindless had decayed skin that was almost grey in colour and blood was splattered on all of their clothes, hands and mouths.

Mia skidded to a stop at the doorway, stunned. Situated right between the Mindless man with bites to his thighs and the Mindless woman with gnashing teeth, was Mia's mother June. It was all so incongruous, a bad dream. She was dressed in a cheery yellow dress and Mia could see the vacuum cleaner in the lounge room where her mother had been working, just like any other day.

But in the next horrible minute, June Cavallari was writhing in pain and screaming as the Mindless tore into her. Georgia had reached out, straining to grab June by the arm to pull her away from them, but their grip held firmly as they sank their yellowing teeth into June's shoulder and arms. Georgia held onto her mother's hand, pulling hard, only for the tug-of-war to unbalance the brawling group. The Mindless woman fell backwards out of the door and down the front porch steps, the force bringing June and the Mindless man with her.

Georgia ran to the front door to try to help June, but stopped in her tracks. Beyond the fallen trio, Mia could make out hundreds of the Mindless coming towards the farm house from the road and the field in front of the house. They were all bloody, dirty and decayed and the closest ones were breaking into their adrenaline-filled run towards the house, having been alerted to the presence of life inside.

June continued to scream as she lay half on the bottom stoop of the front steps. The Mindless woman was tearing into the flesh of her shoulder, making a messy slurping sound while the man was taking chunks out of June's legs.

Mixed in among the sounds of her mother wailing in pain, a high-pitched scream was heard up the stairs to the left of where Mia was standing. Mia tore her eyes away from the front door to the stairwell, where her niece and nephew had run down from their rooms at the sound of all the screams.

Oscar was further up the stairs, crying and screaming in fright as Rosie was kicking against the Mindless man in the ripped suit jacket who had staggered back inside the house. His decayed and exposed jaw bit into Rosie's shoulder, her scream curdling the blood deep inside Mia's veins. Mia gasped in horror as the bright red blood of her niece splattered against the polished wooden bannister.

Suddenly, Mia was pulled backwards with a brutal force. She screamed loudly, thinking it was finally the end before she realised that the large hand on her shoulder actually belonged to her father. George grabbed Mia around the middle and heaved her onto his broad shoulders before taking off towards the back door.

From her position across her father's shoulder, Mia could only watch helplessly as her world crumbled down around her. Georgia had turned from the doorway and made her way up the stairs to help Rosie and Oscar before she disappeared from view. Mia's father carried her through the kitchen and out towards the back door, hesitating for a minute before taking off through the opened door.

As they headed towards the back yard, on her father's shoulder, they passed the laundry room where Mia and Georgia had left the terrified Joan. Mia could see two tattered and decaying Mindless rip open the fresh insides of her sister Joan. Red blood and entrails were splattered everywhere around her sister's now motionless body, staining the cool white tiles of the laundry room she had been left in. Mia let out a scream at the sight of her sister, causing the Mindless to look up at them as they raced out the opened back door.

The Mindless woman's eyes flashed with the bright red rim around the iris and she dropped the blood soaked piece of liver she had been eating. She raised herself from the laundry room floor and began stumbling after Mia and George, her adrenaline starting to kick in. The Mindless woman didn't get far though because as Mia watched in shock, Georgia emerged in the back doorframe with a steel frying pan and swung the heavy cookware at the Mindless woman's head.

The Mindless woman's red-rimmed eyes actually popped out of her crushed head in a bloody streak and she fell face first to the floor. Georgia dropped the frying pan and jumped over the eyeless body, following Mia and her father down the stairs and into the field.

Georgia was covered in bright red blood, it was all over her green t-shirt and jeans; Mia knew that there had been no saving the rest of her family. Georgia was several paces behind George and Mia but as she ran to catch up to her sister and father, she didn't notice the four Mindless flank her from both sides until it was too late.

"Georgia!" Mia screamed, waving wildly at her and trying to get her attention. Mia watched in horror as Georgia turned her body in the direction of the house behind her, pulling one of her father's pistols out of the waistband of her jeans. She pulled the gun up to aim it as the closest Mindless, grasped the handle with both hands and fired. The creature fell, finally dead, on top of her, followed soon afterwards by the other three. Mia watched, sobbing and unable to help, as Georgia struggled under the weight of the Mindless before she disappeared into the tall blades of grass of the field.

It was the last time she had seen her sister alive.

Mia called out her name again, but her father wouldn't stop running. They ran right past August's devoured and bloody body, before they reached the edge of the property, but still George continued to race into the nearby forest. Mia pounded her fists on her father's white shirt, a little too crisp and a little too clean after all of the blood she had just seen.

"Dad! We have to go back! We have to go back!" Mia cried, tears running down her face as she hit her small fists against her father's back. George wouldn't slow down though, no matter what Mia said.

"We can't, Mia. We can't," he told her breathlessly as ran on, dodging tree roots in the forest. Mia sobbed, ceasing her pounding and letting her body trail down her father's shoulders in defeat, her tears falling on the undergrowth he leapt over.

Suddenly, Mia was flying through the air and landed against the thick trunk of a tree. She let out a cry of pain as she crumpled to the forest floor. She looked up, and a couple of feet in front of her was her father in his white shirt and suspenders, trying to fight off one of the Mindless. The Mindless woman was dressed in a long pale blue evening dress with dirt, mud and blood caked up the front of it. Her hair had been pulled into a blonde bun that had fallen out around her decaying face as she bit into George's forearm as he tried to push her off him. The Mindless woman, her strength bolstered by the sight of a fresh meal, had hit George from the side with the force of a car wreck. He struggled to fight against her in his breathless and winded state, despite her slight appearance and inability to move very well in her tight tattered gown.

"Dad!" Mia cried out for her father, who jerked his eyes towards her as she sat crumpled at the base of the tree.

"Run!" he shouted at her, as he turned his eyes back to the Mindless woman ripping into the meat on his arm. She moved to tearing into the left side of his chest with her teeth and Mia saw only red — the red ring around the iris of the Mindless woman, and the bright red blood of her father as the skin on his chest broke open.

Mia squeezed her eyes tight and saw the red of her niece's blood splattering against the bannister, the blood pooling around Joan's dead body, and the blood and brain and eyes shooting out of the woman who Georgia had stopped her with a frying pan.

She couldn't take anymore. Mia opened her eyes and sprang from her crumpled position on the ground, ignoring the wincing pain tearing down her side and the feeling of shattered ribs from landing against the tree. She barely glanced at her father as he was devoured by the Mindless woman in the ball gown, and raced away into the forest.

Mia had run for hours on pure adrenaline. She ran through a river and crossed a rocky stream, raced through the forest fending off low branches and jumping fallen trees, finally coming out on the other side of the woods at the highway. She slowed only for enough time to consider which direction on the highway she would go before she took off towards the city, with the slim hope that if Georgia had survived she would return to her apartment block.

Days later, the tall white apartment block just off a busy intersection in the middle of the city was where Mia had run into Max, Victoria, Jay, Danny, Jacinta and the Feliz family. It was at this apartment that Georgia had once lived, and it was at this apartment that Mia had stayed until the Visitors arrived and the already crazy world had gotten a lot worse.

After all the time Mia waited for her sister with the others, her hope had died. The idea that Georgia had managed to get out alive was almost too good to be true.

"I thought you were dead!" Mia whispered, still holding onto Georgia's arms. They were sitting outside the brick house, sitting on the porch's front steps. The whole setting eerily reminded Mia of her parent's country-style home. It was strange that while Mia had sought out something that reminded her of Georgia, Georgia had sought out something that reminded her of their family home.

"I thought I was too!" Georgia answered, taking her hand. "When that Mindless fell on top of me, I thought it was the end. But I had shot it in the head before it had fallen, so it had met its final end before landing on me. I managed to wriggle my arm with the gun free and shoot the other Mindless that were right behind him. When I got up, I was so covered in blood and shaking, I could barely move or think. There were Mindless everywhere, slowing down after the attack."

"But something happened – they didn't attack me. They just walked right past me. It was crazy! I realised that I was covered in so much of their blood that I must have smelt just like them – dead. I did my best Mindless impression and just walked out of the field in the direction that you and dad went."

"You just walked out of there?" Mia gasped in disbelief, hardly believing her ears.

"Yeah I did," Georgia continued. "I walked into the forest and tried to track you guys down and then I came across dad. It was nearly too much for me, I didn't think I could go on. He was being completely eaten by a woman. I killed her, before I noticed that dad was twisted in a certain way- almost unnaturally. He was pointing and looking to a tree, and when I looked I saw your footprints in the leaves. I knew you had gone that way, and he had left me a signal which gave me hope."

"I tried to find you. I followed your tracks for hours, and then I lost any sign of you when you went in the river. I had no idea where you had gone. It was almost dark by the time I got out of the woods and I searched everywhere and couldn't find you. I ended up walking to our cubby house – you know the one in the tree that dad built us when I was eight? I thought I would find you but you weren't there. I spent the night there before I searched the woods again in the morning for something I may have missed. I searched all day before I came out onto the highway and that's when I saw Valcheck," Georgia motioned to the large, well-built black-haired man that stood behind her on the porch where they sat. Valcheck nodded at them sombrely.

"I asked him if he saw you and he told me you were likely dead. I told him I had to get to the city, thinking that maybe you had gone to my old home but he told me that he had just come from the city and that it was a wasteland, that it was deserted. He convinced me to go with him and we've been together ever since. We met up with others along the way –

Nora, Piccolo and Zeke – the ones who brought you here. There's also Professor Malone too but he's down in the basement. We thought we were all that was left, but I've been searching for you ever since." Georgia finished her story and Mia sat in quiet disbelief, the only sound was the soft rustle of the wind in the trees around them.

"So tell me, what happened to you?" Georgia queried.

As she asked, the wind in the trees began to strengthen, turning from a pleasant breeze into a gust of wind that had the gale force of a hurricane behind it. The wind whipped dust into everyone's eyes and the windows in the house began to rattle with a terrible urgency as if they were about to break.

Mia raised her hands to her eyes, trying to protect them against the sting of the wind. She could barely hear anything above the roar as Valcheck took a protective hold on Georgia's shoulders, pulling her to her feet and into the house with Georgia pulling Mia behind her. They got inside the door and Mia opened her eyes, squinting against the force of the wind. She looked out across the yard, and saw the others falling back to the safety of the porch as well.

Suddenly, the world around them was filled with a shrieking sound – high pitched in quality but coming from some distance away. Mia recognised the shrill sound almost instantly and gasped, running forward from the doorframe to the edge of the porch steps she had just been sitting on.

Victoria and Max came to stand next to Mia and she squinted into the sky and above the treetops, almost hidden by the haze of the dust whisked by the wind, Mia could make out the unmistakable neon blue glow of a ship of the Visitors from another world.

It was almost a day's walk down the road in the direction Victoria, Max, Mia and Jay had come from but there was no mistaking the large, oval-shaped metallic ship as it came in for a landing somewhere beyond the trees of the forest. Round neon blue spheres of light lit up the bottom of the ship, as tubes and pipes let out an unearthly gas that fumed from the ends and caused the air to shimmer. As they continued to land, the futuristic ship let lightning rods lower it to the ground and out of view in the trees, the skyline above the pines bursting with light as small explosives decimated the ground directly underneath the landing zone. As the Visitor's ship lowered to the ground out of view, Mia saw in horror the unmistakable neon blue light of other ships land further down the road they had been walking down. She counted the oval shapes and found herself gasping as she learnt the truth.

A fleet of ten Visitor ships had landed between the highway and the city they had just left. The battle wasn't over – the Visitor's from another planet had sent others to finish the job that the survivors had stopped four months ago.

"What the hell is that?" Georgia asked in disbelief, as the wind settled down again. Unlike the close proximity to the last Visitors' ship they encountered, the air wasn't left with the hum of electricity at this distance. With the breeze back to its normal balmy feeling, it was almost like what they witnessed hadn't even happened and that it was too far away to impact them directly.

"You wanted to know what we have been doing?" Mia asked her sister, turning to look at her. "We've been fighting against that."

CHAPTER 4

The Captain at the control panel inside the ship eased one of the levers forward, sliding the landing rods into position and engaging the gas that was loaded within the ship. The gas was made of a particularly explosive substance that came from the Visitors' home world, and while it was particularly useful for use within their weapons, bombs and landing infrastructure, it was also a very volatile and unstable gas. It made travelling across the gulf of space tricky at times when travelling close to supernovas.

The ship shuddered slightly underneath as the rods met the gas and let out a small explosive burst that created a smooth landing zone on the ground beneath the ship. The concrete and building walls they were landing on were decimated and disappeared into a large hole; the ship smoothly sank into the crater like a bird onto a nest.

Once safely landed, the Commander at the centre of the controls gave a quick shriek to let the Captain know that it was time to unload. The Captain pressed two blue neon buttons that unlatched the entry ways along the side of the ship, where many other Visitors had lain dismembered and dormant inside their pods during flight. Only the Visitors at the control panels were ever awake during long haul space flights.

Looking out past its screen on the panel, the Captain watched as large holes in the ship began to open, making a dense grinding noise as they did so; the sound reverberating through the hollow lightweight metal of the Visitors' ship. There were hundreds of metallic holes opening up to reveal the sleeping Visitors in their pods underneath.

The Commander of the Visitors with its neon green cuff signalled to the other Visitors to complete the landing sequence and then follow it out of the control room and into the main passageway. The Captain at its desk watched as its fellow Visitors began to slide from the holes and land carefully on the ground, their dismembered bodies beginning to melt together to become whole.

Knowing that the disembarking of the Visitors was underway, the Captain at the panel got up from its post and followed the Commander out of the control room. It moved its large legs down the passageway, making sure to lower its head as it passed a ventilation shaft that sometimes caught the Visitors unaware, knocking their large craniums.

The Commander had hit a similar blue button at the end of the passageway and opened the main door to the outside world. The hole slid back like one of the many other metallic holes in the rest of the ship, only it was much larger, and a metallic ramp extended to the ground beneath the ship. The Commander sauntered down the ramp and hit a series of buttons on its glowing green cuff to ignite the weapon installed in it.

Alerted by all the movement, one of the contaminated raced up to the Commander with its adrenaline fuelled desire for a fresh meal. The Commander lazily aimed its gun and fired. The body of the Mindless ripped apart at the seams and splayed itself across the rubble underfoot, missing the Commander with its spray of decay.

The Commander continued to walk purposefully onto the Earth's surface with no regard for the other contaminated humans running up to the Visitors as they were exiting their pods. Each of the Mindless bodies was disposed of quickly by other Visitors as the Commander walked away.

The Captain from the control panel was joined by several others in its team in its pursuit of the Commander and its instructions. They stayed several paces behind, as was protocol, as they ventured into the new world.

The Captain had never been on Earth before and it was actually quite disappointed. The humans had destroyed it with their cement and attitude to a degree that was far worse than the Visitor had ever thought possible. It was an ugly planet; the ground beneath them was hard and grey, and the air smelt much different from its own home world. The Captain found itself missing the gas smell that inhabited its old home and wasn't sure how it would feel resettling here where the air had a crisper quality about it.

The Commander quickly scuttled across the Earth's hard surface and approached its destination – a towering hunk of metal that belonged to the first settlers. The Captain felt a rage deep inside as it approached the burnt out metal and scattered parts, thinking of the Visitors that had been inside when the humans had ruthlessly attacked. The Visitor could hardly believe that the pitiful humans had been able to breach the barriers of their advanced science and kill so many of his species – especially as their planet was almost completely taken over by of contaminated ones.

The Commander sent out a signal for the Visitors to split up and approach the control panel of the decimated ship, taking whatever still operational parts they could find. It then signalled for the Captain to continue to follow as it scuttled around the perimeter of the ship. It continued to move around a large metallic-looking item that the Captain recognised as something that humans had once used for transporting goods. The Captain followed the Commander in rounding the strange rubber and metallic object until it stopped in its tracks and let out a pained shriek.

The Commander stood over the dead body of one of the Visitors. It was slumped to the ground behind the human's strange machine, with dried green brain matter splattered around its head. The Captain could hear the sound of buzzing of earthly insects around its fallen comrade as the body decayed in its position. The metallic cuff all Visitors wore on their wrist was gone from this deceased one, and there was a strange metal item protruded out of the thick muscles of the Visitors neck. It was lodged about four centimetres into the Visitor and it seemed to cut its way in using a series of blades that surrounded the edges of it like teeth. The Captain had never seen such a barbaric weapon in all of its life.

The Commander however showed no fear in wrapping its suction-cupped fingers around the protruding metal casing and pulled it out with all of its might. It struggled to release the weapon from the sticky and congealed matter of the fallen Visitor, as decay had long set in. But the Commander was strong, stronger than death, and eventually dislodged the human's weapon with a wet pull.

The Commander drew the weapon closer to its face and breathed in the heavy scent of the casing through its beady nostrils. The Captain watched as the Commander's eyes closed momentarily before it opened them again and let out an almighty roar unlike those the Visitors usually communicated with.

The Commander was angry.

Ite threw the human's machine towards the Captain, who caught the heavy object gingerly in its suction cupped fingers, unsure of what it might do and unsure of its function. When it didn't whir into life, it did the same thing as the Commander and brought the machine to its own nostrils at the end of its beak.

The Captain breathed in deeply and caught the scent.

It was a smell unlike anything it had either contemplated. It was the smell of skin – human skin. Intrinsically clean, but layered with an acidic sweat, an earthy smell of caked dirt, a tang of metal and a mix of matter that smelt like the Visitor's own blood. It continued to sniff, confirming that it could smell its own essence to the congealed matter on the blade of the weapon. It could identify a homely comfort and strong drive and determination. The smell was indescribable to the Captain, but in its mind it could see the human behind it.

It was a human woman, with brown hair and fierce brown eyes. She was healthy with a strong heart beat and the smell somehow reminded the Captain of home.

The Captain removed the weapon from its beak and dropped it before it suddenly realised that it could smell the human everywhere. She was in the streets around the ship, mixed in the fresh air and turning it stale. She filled every corner of his mind with her scent.

It hated it. It wanted her out of its head.

It turned to the Commander, confused as to what to do next. The Commander looked at it with dark eyes, brimming in an almost neon green that was unusual among any other Visitor than those that led them. There was anger in there, and it was almost as palpable as the human's scent was.

The Commander let out yet another angry groan from deep within its throat and the Captain knew what it had to do, now that it had taken in the human's scent.

It was this human that was behind the failure of the first settlement and the Visitors needed to find her and extract their revenge.

The Captain let out a deep rumbling groan from its own throat, surprised slightly by the animosity behind it, by the hate and the desire for retribution. But the feeling fuelled it and it took one last look at its Commander before it turned and took off as fast as it could down the Earth's strangely hard surface.

CHAPTER 5

"So you guys actually went up against those things and won?" Zeke Mechad asked in disbelief. Zeke was the African man who had held Victoria up at gun point at the marina. He had since apologised for the threats, but only after being prompted by Valcheck Stoll.

The evening had drawn closer and the two groups had retreated inside the bricked manor for the night to discuss the Visitor's second coming. Jay stood at attention on the front porch, keeping watch for any nearby Visitors who may be searching for them. They seemed to have landed quite a distance away, so they considered themselves relatively safe for the night.

But they wouldn't be for long.

The front door was ajar, and Victoria could see Jay within earshot squinting out into the darkening night. The cool forest air breezed into the room and tasted sweet in Victoria's throat, but was mingled with the kind of electrical feeling that comes just before a storm.

The two groups sat around in the building's living area, which had hard-wood floors and dusty Persian-style carpets that layered and lined the centre of the sitting area. Several dusty chaise lounges had been pushed together into a circle that the groups shared. Victoria, Max and Nora sat on one of the lounges while Georgia sat holding the tear-streaked Mia's hands on the other. Zeke lounged casually on the third sofa next to Piccolo, while Valcheck paced the room behind them.

In their hurried discussions after the arrival of the Visitors, Victoria, Max, Mia and Jay had been properly introduced to the group and to the three who had held them captive. Victoria had been right to guess Zeke Mechad as being ex-military, as he had explained that he had been a soldier before the contamination of the world. His platoon had been overrun by a horde of Mindless during a planned attack to take back the capital, and without his fearless commander he had been left without order and without direction. He had come across Valcheck and Georgia just outside the city not long after Georgia and Mia had escaped the battle of their own and had taken on his new role as a grunt with pride.

Tough as nails and willing to do anything, Zeke had the air of an undisciplined loner about him as he lounged comfortably and chomped on the end of a cigar like he didn't have a care in the world.

Victoria glared at him as he inhaled in the smoke of the cigar, lighting up the ashy base. He might not have a care in the world, but she did, and without a lot of the proper assistance available in this new world, she wasn't going to take any chances.

"We sure did," Victoria answered, focusing her attention instead on the cigar that Zeke was smoking. "Can you please put that out?" she asked, moving her eyes to indicate what she meant.

"Why?" Zeke quizzed, blowing a puff of smoke out of his mouth and into the air. Victoria's eyes narrowed as the smoke dissipated in the room.

"I told you I am pregnant," she told him matter-of-factly. Georgia and Valcheck, who hadn't been on the beach to hear Max discuss his wife's condition, froze in their tracks, surprised by the fact she was having a baby with the world in the condition it was in. Slowly, they began to regain their initial composure.

"And like I told you, we can fix that …" Zeke said long and slow, but making no move to put out his cigar.

"Put it out," Valcheck said strongly from his place behind the couches. He had also been smoking his own cigar, but instantly he put it out in the nearest ashtray. Zeke did what he said, stubbing the cigar out in an ashtray on the floor next to the lounge that was filled to the brim with butts. Once it was firmly out, Zeke put the rest of the unlit cigar back into his shirt pocket for later.

Valcheck Stoll was without a doubt the leader of the group and both his physical and intellectual strength brought and held the group together. He was a large stocky man with well-built muscles and a pale complexion that offset his jet black hair, slicked back into a pompadour style. He had a matching well-groomed goatee but he constantly wore a hardened look on his face and spoke with a thick accent that suggested a birthright in the north east that had its roots firmly planted in Russian heritage.

Valcheck had been a fire-fighter in the city when the contamination had first occurred and had been called to a situation in a dank apartment complex on the edge of the city. He had been caught up battling the Mindless inside the apartment while it raged from the suburbs across town where victim one Ian Peters had lived. Valcheck had been the only person to escape unscathed.

With no family or ties whatsoever, Valcheck was married to his job and had thrown himself into helping people around the city, but eventually as the contamination continued it was apparent that there were no longer any uncontaminated humans left to be saved. He had packed up and left via the highway, bumping into Georgia in the woods. He had been instantly attracted to the slim brunette with blood-soaked clothes and wild eyes and convinced her to come with him, honestly believing that after seeing the city in ruins that the sister she had been searching for would be long dead.

So they had walked and fought and survived. They had met up with Zeke first on the highway before running into the others along the way. Nora had been next, found hiding in the boot of an abandoned car, furiously trying to escape.

She had introduced herself as Nora Dallas but she had both a mysterious and familiar air about her.

"I'm sure I've seen you somewhere before," Victoria told Nora. "Are you sure you haven't been into the city?"

Nora arched one of her perfectly plucked eyebrows in response. "Not since I escaped in the outbreak. I moved around a lot beforehand, maybe you saw me there once or twice," she said off-handedly, waving the idea away with a perfectly manicured hand that seemed out of place at the end of the world.

Everything about Nora seemed out of place, but also somehow complete – she was an enigma. She hadn't offered much about her past unlike the others, and she was difficult to read. She was very attractive with her thick black hair, blemish-free porcelain skin and blinding blue eyes and she surprised everyone by being very feminine in appearance but tough in nature. Victoria had already seen her down two fingers of straight whiskey since they had arrived and had puffed away on her own cigar with the fervour of a woman who enjoyed her vices.

In the quick rounds of getting to know the group, Victoria had instantly placed Nora as the dangerous liaison, and the one to watch.

After the group had welcomed Nora into the fold, they had started setting up shelter in the country manor where they currently resided. They completed their family by meeting Piccolo and Professor Malone from the nearby university shortly afterwards.

Piccolo Mein was the Asian man who had accompanied the others at the hostage situation, and was the youngest of the group at twenty-three years old. Piccolo had been a student at a nearby university, accepted under a scholarship because he was a gifted athlete and a fast runner. He had explained that when the contamination had ripped through his school, Piccolo had been in a biomedical engineering class and had survived in the university laboratory with his professor and a female student named Louise. Piccolo had been the one who scavenged supplies for his small group because he was the only one who could outrun the adrenaline-fuelled Mindless. But eventually the Mindless had followed Piccolo back into the lab.

Piccolo and the Professor had been the only ones to escape. A flicker of shame and sadness crossing Piccolo's face as he mentioned the loss of Louise.

Victoria understood. They were all haunted by those they had lost, especially if it had been their actions that had started the chain of events.

The group hadn't met the Professor yet, as he was apparently down in the windowless basement working on an experiment and was known to disappear for days at a time. Piccolo had explained he was trying to work on a cure to turn the Mindless back into humans, which is what occupied his time.

"With the Visitors back again, he's got bigger things to worry about," Max told Piccolo, shaking Victoria from her thoughts and pulling her back into the present.

"I think it's safe to say we all do," Nora answered him.

"The question is what can we do about these Visitors?" Valcheck asked in his thick accent.

"Well, we have those cuff guns but we only have four of them," Victoria answered. After the Visitors had landed and the group had moved indoors, Victoria had explained how she had been entranced by one of the Visitors and discovered that they could be killed by their own weapons – both by the Mindless they had created and the guns on the cuffs that they wore. She had even shown the group the gun dropping out of her own cuff which she wore on her wrist every day since the attack.

"There's no way that will be enough to take them all down," said Georgia who was still holding Mia's hand tightly, afraid to let go of her sister now that she had her back in her life. "There had to have been dozens of ships that landed between here and the city, and that's not even taking into account ships that may have landed in other cities!"

"We can't just give up. We fought them once, we can fight them again," Victoria spoke to Georgia directly in an even tone. "We keep moving. If there are others, we do the same thing. They need to know that they just can't come down to our planet and take whatever they want. Like it or not, we are the new world order. We are all that is left and we didn't survive this long against the Mindless to just lie down and take it when another threat comes along."

"There might be others out there doing the same thing as us right now," Piccolo piped up, sitting a bit straighter in his seat. "People in other countries even, we can't be the only ones left. If things get back online and back to the way they used to be we can't be the ones who sat in the corner and did nothing."

Piccolo's optimism for getting the world back together was not necessarily shared, but the group around Victoria now were fighters. She didn't see them backing out of a fight just because things got tough.

"I'm aching for a good fight," Zeke grinned, proving Victoria's thought to be true.

"Slow down Zeke. We need a plan. Four of those guns are still not enough to take them all down," Georgia's bright blue eyes flashed as she looked around at her group who were more than gearing up for a fight.

"Then we're just going to have to get more," Victoria said, matching Zeke's bright smile as she began forming a plan.

"If we get more, Professor Malone might be able to help us," Piccolo offered, looking sideways at Victoria.

The group looked at each other and took in their surroundings. They were only nine people. Two families that barely knew each other but were forced together with a common friend and a common threat. Victoria could practically feel the energy radiating from each and every one of them and she saw the familiar glint of fight in their eyes.

"Looks like we're going to war then," Valcheck declared.

*****

"Fascinating," mumbled Professor Buddy Malone as he shifted the spectacles further up the brim of his nose. "Absolutely fascinating."

The group had descended downstairs into the basement of the house to find the Professor, and Victoria felt like she had been catapulted into the laboratory of a mad scientist. Work benches covered over half of the basement floor, and on every surface was a piece of equipment, research or paper piles that confirmed the impression you were in the presence of an intelligent mind. Bunsen burners, Petri dishes and beakers sat next to sheets of slightly transparent paper marked with symbols and equations; a microscope was set up in one corner with marked slides piled carefully next to it, and different equipment made of steel, glass and wire covered many surfaces. Victoria couldn't name half of the equipment she saw on the benches but guessed it helped to analyse blood and bodily fluids given the Professor was seeking a cure for the Mindless.

On one end of the basement was a large whiteboard covered with equations scribbled with faded markers, and in the middle of the clearest section of basement was a large steel gurney on wheels with straps fashioned to it where arms and legs would rest. A steel cage in the far corner of the room was covered in a large white paint-splattered sheet and it reminded Victoria of old horror movies about monsters being created from body parts.

Professor Buddy Malone was an interesting man. He was rather short and had long wild hair that was as white as a dove. He had golden brown eyes framed by dark eyelashes that blinked out from beneath his classic black round spectacles.

Georgia had introduced the new group to the Professor before Valcheck spoke up and told him about the new Visitors that had arrived on Earth.

"We've dealt with them before," Victoria spoke up. "We battled them and were able to get this weapon off them." She showed him the cuff that she wore on her wrist and clicked a few buttons that released it from her arm. As it dropped from her wrist it made a soft whooshing noise and she caught it in her other palm. Her wrist felt strange without the cuff on – warmer somehow. The metal of the cuff had always been cold to touch and wearing it had not been any different. She'd gotten used to the kiss of cold metal against her skin and it felt strange to not have it pressed against her.

Victoria passed the cuff to Professor Malone and he adjusted his glasses, fawning over the metal in fascination.

"Here, look at this," she told him and pushed a series of buttons that released the gun from its bed deep within the cuff. The gun connected itself together like a puzzle in a series of metallic clinks and Professor Malone watched it with deep curiosity.

"This gun absolutely obliterates everything in its path," Max explained, standing next to Victoria. "For every biological entity it causes an implosion, in on itself. It's quite oozy, but it works against them."

"The only issue is …" Victoria continued where Max had left off. They had been leaving out a very important piece of information. "These Visitors can regenerate themselves. We've seen them regrow limbs that were cut off, even parts of heads. A new hand or leg just shoots out in its place, or the part seals over."

"If they can regenerate, how did you defeat them last time then?" Georgia asked, worried.

"I learnt something very valuable when they captured me. They can be turned, just like us. They can become the Mindless," Victoria answered.

"But isn't that worse? Not only are they regenerative Visitors from another planet who we have absolutely no information on, but isn't turning them into unthinking, fast killing machines even worse?" Nora asked, disbelief on her beautiful face.

"When we turn, we die don't we? We can't think, we can't feel, we aren't anything anymore. The things we used to do, we can't do. The only thing we can do is run, attack, and eat. Right?" Victoria asked the group.

"Theoretically," Professor Malone said, still examining the cuff and the gun attached. He pushed his glasses up his nose once more and looked up towards Victoria. "I'm currently researching the Mindless and what happens when they turn. Neurologically speaking, the brain is still functioning, but it has been contaminated to the point that only the hypothalamus functions."

"What is the hypothalamus area?" asked Max in response.

"It's typically the part of the brain where aggressive behaviours come from – behaviours such as premeditated violence, as well as the part of the brain that controls sleep and hunger. In the Mindless brain, this part is the only part that still functions and doesn't rot away, though it is compromised to a point that the aggression and the hunger becomes a compulsion, rather than an act of pre-meditation," the Professor explained. "I've learnt that that Mindless brain lights up in the hypothalamus area in particular but the contamination starts to rot the rest of the brain. I've been trying to find a cure with Piccolo's assistance."

"And how exactly did you study this?" Victoria asked suspiciously, arching one of her eyebrows. She knew where this was going, and she wasn't sure she liked the answer.

"I have many methods available to me," Professor Malone answered, cagily. "In order to defeat one's enemy one has to know it first."

"Professor Malone has ensured us his practices are safe. This is why Piccolo helps him," Georgia answered, aware of Victoria's suspicions and sticking up for the Professor.

Victoria paused for a while, not sure what to say. She knew that the Professor's methods were without a doubt dangerous, and she wasn't sure how to feel about the idea of these tests. She'd been strongly opposed to animal testing back when scientists did so, but she had been conflicted by the strong results they had yielded. It sounded like the Professor was utilising the Mindless in a similar way, and it concerned her.

But on the other hand, the research into the brain functioning of the Mindless and the connection with the Visitors was important to know.

"So, how do we use this information to our advantage then?" she asked, finally deciding to look past Professor Malone's practices.

"Well, the Visitors must have a similar brain because they aren't immune to this contamination," Max said, piecing it together. "And it's true that when they become the Mindless Visitors then they are more powerful than the human Mindless, but because their brains don't function in the way that they used to it also can't regenerate. This means that they can be killed in exactly the same way that the Mindless can be – with a shot or deep blow to the head."

Max brandished his hand towards the otherworldly gun that Professor Malone was still holding.

"This weapon decimates the Mindless and seems to have the same effect on a Mindless Visitor. So yes, while Mindless Visitors are more dangerous, they can be killed easier than if they were simply Visitors. Their ships are also destroyable. There seems to be some kind of gas leaking out the sides of it, so we were able to destroy it with a grenade. We do have to get close enough to do so though."

"Very interesting ..." Professor Malone continued in his study of the cuff. "It is very interesting that they seem to share a similar biological makeup as we do, as well as a similar type of combustive gas."

"The Visitors started this Mindless contamination of the world, so I guess they based it on their own research?" offered Max.

"How do you know that these Visitors are the ones who started the outbreak?" Georgia asked suspiciously, her arms folded over her chest.

"As I said I was captured by the Visitors when they took a friend of ours, a member of the group named Ian Peters. They sought Ian out specifically because he turned out to be victim zero. When they came for him, he was screaming about how he had been abducted by them, and how he knew them years earlier at the start of the outbreak. They must have put something in him – something that was meant to start the outbreak and keep it spreading – because he was immune to the Mindless contagion," Victoria explained.

"He was immune? What do you mean?" Professor Malone asked quickly, raising his spectacles again. He seemed to play with them a lot when he was deep in thought.

"I saw his back and it was covered in bites, bruises, everything. He'd been bitten so many times, but he was completely fine," Victoria said. "His eyes reflected a neon blue ring – exactly like one that the Visitors have. He must have been contaminated and started the outbreak and they came back looking for him specifically to finish him off because the outbreak never would."

"How did he start the outbreak?" Professor Malone quizzed.

"We never found out. He kept it a secret from us the whole time, and we thought he was just introverted and nervous. When the Visitors arrived he just panicked and then he was taken. I tried to help and was taken too, but then he was killed and I escaped," Victoria's voice lowered.

"And that was when you made this discovery, that the Visitors can be turned into the Mindless?" asked Georgia.

"Yes," answered Victoria. "And also where I saw the Visitors use their own weapon against the Mindless Visitors. They know what they are doing and how to do it."

"Well how many of these weapons do you have?" Professor Malone asked, pressing the button with ease to close up the gun back into the cuff and then balancing the cuff in his right hand.

"We have four of them from our last battle," Mia answered, piping up for the first time since she spoke with Georgia about where she had been.

"And how many ships do you think arrived?"

"Ten maybe, between here and the city," Mia replied.

"I think I can devise a weapon out of these cuffs with the similar capabilities of a bomb. You said you blew up their ships before with a grenade, didn't you?" Professor Malone discussed his idea with the group. "Do you have any more?"

"No, we don't have any more grenades. We only found a few in an overturned military vehicle." Max explained.

"If I have some time – and some more of these cuffs – I should be able to create a device that will have a similar effect as the explosion that the grenades caused. If we can put these under each of the ten ships where the gas comes out, we can get rid of these Visitor ships once and for all," Professor Malone finished.

"Do you really think it will work?" Georgia asked.

"There's only one way to find out," Victoria replied. "It's either try it this way or sit on our hands and wait for the Visitors to find us and take over the Earth."

"I'm in," Valcheck piped up in his thick accent.

"Me too," said Nora while Piccolo nodded his head in agreement.

"Let's give them Hell!" Zeke said enthusiastically, pumping his fist into the air.

"So how do we do this then?" Georgia asked, crossing her arms in front of her chest.

"I think I have just the idea …" Professor Malone said with a smile.

CHAPTER 6

Piccolo Mein sat in the driver's side of a big rig truck, navigating the monstrous vehicle slowly along the highway. The need to drive it slowly was symbiotic to his lack of truck driving skills – he was usually the runner, not the driver.

Sitting next to Piccolo in the passenger side was Jay Welles, the quiet dark-haired man who had travelled with the other group. His long black hair was pulled back off his face and worn under his grey beanie, and he was wrapped up with his black leather jacket, black fingerless gloves and a woolly grey scarf.

Jay hadn't said much in the group's first interactions together, but Piccolo hadn't either, beyond their introductions. He looked like a classic cool guy, all style and strength, but he projected the image of a thoughtful type and that suited Piccolo just fine. Piccolo was used to being perceived in a certain way and had grown to accept that was more about the other person's flaws rather than his own.

Piccolo had simply learnt to surprise people.

It had only been during his later school years that he had begun to defy people's expectations. Growing up, his parents had always put a lot of emphasis on his studies so he'd developed an intelligent mind, but after a while he'd had enough of the general prejudice against his Asian background. So one year after summer vacation, at a time when people usually reinvent themselves, he did something out of the ordinary – he tried out for the track team.

He started running, and he never looked back.

Piccolo had always been a fast runner and it had been his preferred method of physical activity. Everything about Piccolo was fast where it counted – his intelligence meant he could formulate a plan quickly, and his wiry body meant he could spring into action quickly. Hell, even when he was bullied he was able to put an end to it quickly with a fast and witty reply.

Eventually, Piccolo started winning competitions on the track and people started taking notice. He developed strong and lean muscles and suddenly he was invited to parties hosted by the jocks and the cool kids. He was popular and had defied all of the prejudicial expectations these same kids had bullied him with earlier in his school years.

He knew that these same bullies were still somewhere inside them though, so he had learnt to be quiet and calculating. He only really spoke when he needed to, and he used the quiet to his advantage. Speak less, listen more worked well for him.

When Piccolo moved on to university he outwardly hadn't changed much, and being an observer of life made him appear to be an introvert. However, the way the university system worked, people from his classes never saw him on the track and never knew the extent of his talents, nor did they really care. Because of this, Piccolo found himself in a rare position of having heaps of friends from his track team, but none in his actual classes.

He was back to being nobody, but it suited him just fine.

However, there was really only one person that Piccolo wanted to be a 'somebody' for and her name was Louise Reynolds.

Louise Reynolds had a pretty face with a speckling of freckles and a carefree smile. She tossed her long auburn curls over her shoulder when she spoke to boys and wore tight clothing that hugged her slim figure. Piccolo had seen her around the university campus often as he always looked out for her. She wasn't easy to miss as she was always laughing and joking, and putting her slender fingers on the broad shoulders of handsome men.

She was flirty, flighty and popular in the halls, but Piccolo knew that Louise was just like him. That something more was buried underneath her shiny surface.

He thought this way because Piccolo never saw Louise joke or flirt with any of the guys in their biomedical engineering class, and he always saw her taking studious notes. She was specialising in molecular biology and its uses within medical engineering and was fascinated with science in general.

This was why Piccolo sat up and took mental notes on Louise. She was not only smart and beautiful, but in the times that he had sat behind her in class and burnt a hole in her shoulders with his mystified stare, he had also noticed two jet black dyed streaks running underneath the bottom of her auburn curls. Because of this, Piccolo knew that there was more to Louise, she was just as calculating about the person she presented to the world as he was.

Piccolo desperately wanted to know the person underneath the perfectly curled hair– the person with the jet-black streaks.

Despite his desperation to make contact with Louise, Piccolo had not worked up the courage to talk to her, at least not until that fateful day when everything changed and the outbreak had occurred.

They had been sitting in class with Professor Malone lecturing them on developing biomechanics when a student Piccolo had seen around campus burst into the room from one of the side doors that led to the school's main corridor. He was dark-skinned and dressed casually in dark jeans, a t-shirt and an opened black cardigan, but he was puffing and out of breath.

"There's a riot!" he cried to the class before he ducked out of the same door. The students started chatting excitedly, breaking the silence of the room. Some stood up from their desks and tried to look out of the window, and some started packing up their things and heading for both the door and the emergency exit on the other side of the lecture podium that Professor Malone was standing at.

"Alright, alright, settle down!" Professor Malone shouted over the din of his class from the front of the room, waving his arms in a lowering motion. Suddenly the noise of the classroom was pierced with a loud and constant alarm, which Piccolo recognised as the school's emergency evacuation alert.

Almost as one, the class hurriedly made for the doors at the front of the room, some of them grabbing their books and bags while others simply took off for the exits. Piccolo had been sitting at the back of the room to the right – a position he had taken to better sneak glances at Louise throughout the class – so he calmly grabbed his backpack from the side of the floor and followed the crush to the front doors.

Louise had been just as slow in rising from her seat. Usually these kinds of evacuations were just a drill, and there was no way she was going to break one of her huge heels trying to get out for what was likely a false alarm. Piccolo manoeuvred to catch up to her and managed to sidle in next to her in the throng of their classmates.

"I wonder if it's actually a riot?" Piccolo casually mentioned to her, using the proximity to strike up the conversation he had longed for but had always failed at – usually falling over himself every time he tried.

"I dunno, that guy could have been one of the drama students," Louise answered as they shuffled towards the door. "You know how they like to get worked up over things like that and make it as real as possible."

Professor Malone was still standing at his desk, ensuring his students departed the classroom appropriately before he left himself. He was barking directions to his class about where to go to meet at the closest emergency evacuation point.

As Piccolo and Louise walked out into the main corridor, Piccolo opened his mouth to say something but struggled to articulate the appropriate words that would make him sound both cool and intelligent. Louise used the moment of silence to grab the arm of a girl who had been moving with the crowd down the corridor. Piccolo recognised her as Charlie, one of Louise's friends, who had similarly curled blonde hair and wore a light coloured sweater and artfully ripped jeans.

"What's going on?" Louise asked Charlie as they stepped to the side and away from the crush of people charging down the corridor. Piccolo was pushed out of earshot of the girls and ended up on the other side of the corridor against a wall. People of all backgrounds crushed by him down the hall and through the double glass doors that exited out of the buildings; they were students casually dressed in jeans and sweaters, professors dressed in pencil skirts, crisp business pants, and a few older men in university-approved tweed jackets. Everyone moved towards the exit like a herd of lemmings.

Suddenly, Piccolo heard several screams echo through the tiled corridor and he looked in the opposite direction of the glass doors. He could barely see anything over the moving bodies that flowed passed him, but he thought he could make out the riot at the end of the corridor and was surprised that this wasn't a false alarm.

The people in the riot were pushing against each other like they were in a mosh pit, being thrown against the walls and the floor. Some were trying to escape, to keep moving, but others were jumping on top of them with a supernatural agility, attacking those trying to get away and forcing them backwards into the crowd.

The throng of people moving towards the exit started picking up speed when they heard the screams behind them, and the group cleared a little around Piccolo as they passed. That was when he saw it for what it truly was.

An Asian woman with black round-rimmed glasses was lying on the floor, trying to pull herself up the corridor. An older teacher in a grey skirt, blouse and heels jumped on top of her with a velocity that was not expected of a women in such a demure business-like outfit. Piccolo saw a glint of red in her eyes as she ripped at the Asian woman's t-shirt at the back, pulling it apart with ease. She gnashed her teeth furiously and bent down to bite into the woman, tearing through her skin with her teeth.

Piccolo gasped in horror as the Asian woman cried out in pain and shock, blood flowing from her back onto the floor as the teacher bit into her with a savage urgency.

Piccolo slowly realised these similar horrific actions were taking place all around the corridor. He saw a trendy man with short blonde hair pushed up against the wall of the corridor by another man in a checked shirt, his brown hair pulled into a short ponytail at the top of his head. The checked-shirt man was holding onto the trendy man with inhuman strength and biting into his shoulder as his victim screamed. Blood mixed with the red checked shirt in a horrifying burst of colour. A fat kid dressed in all black came barrelling towards a woman with brightly coloured hair, knocking her to the ground and tearing into her like she was a hamburger.

"What the hell is going on?" Professor Malone cried, emerging from the front doors of his classroom opposite to where Piccolo was standing wide-eyed and taking in the scene at the end of the hall. The urgency in his voice pulled Piccolo from his stupor and he realised that the crowd had thinned and he was standing with Louise and Charlie, who had spent the entire time talking on the opposite side of the corridor and were also only now just taking in the horrifying scene.

Piccolo looked back towards the carnage and saw the man in the checked skirt and ponytail looking in their direction – Professor Malone's cry was drawing attention to them. The man's brown eyes glinted in the sunlight and reflected a perfect ring of red around the iris in his eyes. He immediately let go of the trendy man he had been biting, the man sliding down to the tiled floor, whimpering and trying to stem the flow of blood pouring from his neck and shoulder.

The teacher in the pencil skirt and heels had also been alerted to their presence and looked up from where she knelt on top of the Asian woman, now lying face down and unmoving on the floor. The woman's back had been ripped open completely, and all Piccolo could see was a mass of blood, flesh and a few splinters of the back of her ribcage and spine poking up through all of the red. The teacher had blood all over her mouth and the same red ring around the irises in her eyes.

The adrenaline that was pumping through the teacher and the checked-shirt man filled the room like static electricity and Piccolo started backing up, feeling their pent up energy like the preparation runners have before taking off on a competitive sprint.

"Run!" Piccolo cried as they sprang forward towards them with a fierce velocity, gnashing their teeth. Piccolo was ahead of Charlie, Louise, and Professor Malone quickly as they were much slower than he was with their heels and older age. Just as he had started to sprint, he knew he couldn't leave them behind in this melee – especially not Louise – and he slowed his pace and looked behind him.

Professor Malone was coming up behind him, running as fast as he could, but Louise and Charlie were running at a completely inadequate slow pace, holding hands and tottering on their ridiculous heels. Charlie was slightly behind Louise, and Piccolo watched in horror as the checked-shirt man and teacher reached her easily. They grabbed her from both sides and took her down, Louise dropping her hand as Charlie fell and stumbled forward a few spaces, turning back and trying to reach for her friend.

"Charlie!" Louise squealed in a high-pitched voice as she kept her hand outstretched, tears running down her face. Charlie screamed and continued to reach out to Louise as the checked-shirt man and teacher ripped into her. The checked-shirt man bit into the flesh of her shoulders, tearing off a chunk of flesh and spraying blood all over the gleaming white tiled floors of the school hallway. The teacher ripped into Charlie's back like she did with the Asian woman, tearing her clothes and her skin like tissue paper.

Piccolo looked beyond the carnage and saw that the trendy man with the blood flowing from his neck and shoulder was heading towards them rapidly. His eyes now glinted with the same red ring around the iris as the others had. Closely behind him was the fat kid dressed in black.

They were all coming for them.

In a split second decision, Piccolo took off back towards Louise and Charlie. He covered the space between them in a few fast bounds and in one fluid motion he wrapped his strong arms around Louise's tiny waist. He lifted her up easily into his arms and spun her around to face the other way. Louise doubled over slightly under the pressure, falling forward across his arms.

Piccolo hiked her up to an easier angle and took off running down the corridor again, his stride falling a little behind due to Louise's albeit very light extra weight. Louise was screaming and crying out to Charlie, but Piccolo wouldn't let her go.

Ahead of them, Professor Malone had opened a door in the corridor and was gesturing wildly at them to hurry. Piccolo upped the pace a little and ran through the door into a smaller darkened corridor. Professor Malone followed in behind him and shut and locked the door as Piccolo placed Louise back down on to her own feet. Louise's knees buckled and she collapsed onto the floor on her knees, crying.

Piccolo turned his attention to helping Professor Malone move one of the steel bookshelves that lined the darkened corridor into place by the door. They were rough with the movement of the furniture and several books that lined the shelf fell out and landed with a thud around the whimpering Louise.

Piccolo could hear the kid and the trendy man slam into the corridor side of the door and the frosted glass of the window on the door cracked slightly under their pressure. The door made splintering and thudding sounds as they tried to get in. Piccolo and Professor Malone pulled the bookshelf finally into place and then the Professor indicated up the passageway.

"We can get to my office up here. It has a window that we can get through and out onto the courtyard and get out of here," he said. Professor Malone started striding up the corridor leading the way.

Piccolo stooped and grabbed Louise by the hand, pulling her to her feet. She was still crying, but she rose with him.

"You need to take off your heels Louise. I can't carry you everywhere," Piccolo told her.

"But … these are designer!" Louise sniffled, wiping her hand across her nose.

"And they look great, but we may need you to run. Take them off," he instructed her. Louise nodded slowly and sadly and gripped Piccolo's arm with one hand as she bent down and slid her fingers into the back of her heels, sliding them off. Once they were off, she bent down and picked them up and held them tightly. Piccolo started walking fast down the corridor and held her hand – a hand he had wanted to hold for so long – bringing her with him.

They followed Professor Malone down the darkened corridor and through a woodened panelled door on the right. Piccolo had never been in Professor Malone's office before but it looked like any other university professor's office. There was a deep wooden desk covered in papers, pens, pads and an office computer, and there was a leather desk chair seated behind one side of the desk and two smaller guest chairs on the other side. Facing the desk was a large metal bookshelf that took up the entire wall and was rammed full of books, papers, folders, lab equipment and a plant or two. A large window took up the outer wall and looked out onto the green courtyard outside the building.

Professor Malone was looking out through one half-closed venetian blind, and as Piccolo approached with Louise he saw that the carnage inside was being easily matched with the carnage in the courtyard. People were everywhere, running and escaping, attacking others, fighting others off. Those who had turned into the same red-eyed Mindless humans were attacking whoever they came across and tearing people to shreds. Blood and entrails splattered the grass of the courtyard and the cement footpaths and the walls of the building.

There was no way they would be able to escape through the courtyard.

Louise let out a whimper and dropped her expensive shoes with a clutter on Professor Malone's office floor. She buried her face into Piccolo's chest and clutched his arm while still holding his hand with the other.

Piccolo could barely breathe. He was finally having the time and interaction with Louise that he longed for, but he was surrounded by death and horror.

If it counted as a first date, it wasn't going well.

"There's no way we're going to get out until this dies down," Professor Malone told them, dropping his hands from the venetian blinds and adjusting his glasses, thinking.

"Do you know somewhere we can go where we can hide and ride this out?" Piccolo asked his biomedical engineering professor who pondered where they can go.

"There is access to a lab from Professor Marty's office just down the hall. Marty's been having problems with his wife recently and has actually been staying in the lab on the down low. It's for his own academic experimentations, but he keeps food and water in there. We can stay there until its safe."

"Let's go then," said Piccolo as Professor Malone ran over to his desk, grabbed a framed photo of his wife and two children and then led the way out of his office. Piccolo and Louise followed into the darkened corridor and down the hall. Professor Malone ducked into a door on the left just as a deafening creak followed by a thud filled the room. The steel bookcase they had used as a barricade had been pushed over by the adrenaline-fuelled force of the trendy man and the fat kid in black.

Piccolo and Louise stood stunned for a second as they watched the fat kid try to get up from having fallen over with the bookshelf. The door was cracked and splintered all up one side and they could see the trendy man clawing to get in, making a groaning sound as he did so.

"Come on!" Professor Malone cried, pulling Piccolo and Louise once again from their stupor. They hurried into Professor Marty's office and shut and locked the door behind them. Professor Malone pointed to a separate door on the other side of the office and Louise hurried to that door while Piccolo and Professor Malone each took a side of Professor Marty's desk and used it to barricade the door once more.

They took off after Louise into the lab, locking and barricading the door behind them yet again. Piccolo looked around the lab for a weapon and was happy to find a tray of surgical equipment on one of the laboratory's benches. Professor Marty was a biology professor and they regularly worked with dissections in his class, so scalpels and other sharp surgical tools were readily available throughout the laboratory drawers. Piccolo gave several tools to both Louise and Professor Malone while keeping some for himself.

"What do you want me to do with this?" Louise asked horrified as Piccolo handed her own sealed pack of surgical utensils.

"Defend yourself," said Piccolo.

Louise started shaking her head vigorously. "No, no, no! I can't do that!" she cried. Piccolo grabbed hold of both of her shoulders and stooped slightly to look directly into the light blue eyes that he had dreamed of looking into for so long. She stopped shaking her head and looked straight back at him.

"I can't lose you Louise," Piccolo told her with all the sincerity he could muster. He didn't know what he would do if he lost her to one of them. Louise took him in and regarded him for a second that felt like forever. Her eyes softened slightly and Piccolo felt like Heaven had opened up before him. She nodded slowly in response.

"If I'm not interrupting," said Professor Malone as he cleared his throat awkwardly. "We need to hide and stay quiet. They shouldn't be able to get through both doors and if we stay quiet they may not be able to find us. We will resurface when we can and get out of here, but in the meantime take cover and get ready to defend yourself."

Piccolo nodded at the Professor, and Malone walked over to the other side of the lab. He slowly flipped a steel silvery gurney onto its side as quietly as possible and ducked down behind it, settling in to barricade himself from an impending attack. Piccolo ushered Louise to sit with him and they sat behind one of the steel stationary laboratory benches. They sat side by side, Louise barefoot and still clutching his arm, resting her head on his shoulder.

Piccolo took in her curly auburn hair, now wild from the run, and leaned his own head against hers for comfort. He could hardly breathe from being in such close proximity to her, and he could hardly believe everything that was happening.

It was just his luck that he ended up with the most beautiful girl he had ever seen on the day that Earth happened to stand still.

Piccolo, Louise and Professor Malone stayed in the laboratory for days. Waiting, barely breathing, for time to pass and the danger to die away.

But the danger would never end, and Piccolo learnt that soon enough.

Thinking about Louise was dangerous for Piccolo nowadays, but despite everything that had happened in those first apocalyptic weeks, that first day of horror and the days that followed had been the best time of Piccolo's life.

He had spent the better part of the week with Louise and Professor Malone in that laboratory and he had learnt so much about her in that time. Louise told him about her home life, her family, and why she was studying biomedical engineering in the first place. She told him about her brother, who was the radical black sheep of the family who played bass guitar in a rock band, and about the horses she rode when she was younger, and why she had decided to get black streaks in her hair in order to annoy her conservative and social-climbing parents.

Piccolo remembered every detail of her stories, every look she gave him, and every touch of her hand against his arm. He loved her more deeply in those moments of grave danger than he ever did before.

And he started to feel that she had come to love him.

But then everything changed. They left the laboratory and moved to the offices. Piccolo went on supply runs to the cafeteria and eventually Louise began to grow restless. She and the Professor were never fast enough to contribute in the way that Piccolo did and she began to snap under the pressure of waiting, of feeling helpless. She had a family and a life that she was sure were gone, but she grew annoyed when Piccolo and the Professor would turn down her suggestions that they should leave the campus so she could find them. The courtyard was always too full of the Mindless and the university gates had closed, locking the wandering humans in with them. They had always agreed for their own protection, but Louise grew tired of having her ideas and her feelings rejected.

And then when Piccolo unintentionally led a small horde of Mindless into their secure area after a scouting mission, he had watched the love of his life die at the hands of the dark-skinned student that had burst into their classroom, warning them all of the riot on the day of the outbreak. He still wore his dark jeans, t-shirt and black cardigan, but his dark skin was rotting and shredded, his eyes rimmed with red.

Piccolo blamed himself – he was devastated and upon his escape with Professor Malone, resolved to never discredit anyone else's opinions or plans. He vowed that he would never lose another person again.

Now, he was sitting in the truck with Jay Welles and he was as silent as a graveyard. Piccolo really wanted to like this man – he seemed like someone he probably would have hung out with back when the Earth had still been a vibrant array of life. Moving together in this truck, Piccolo knew that they needed to get the conversation going, otherwise it would be hard to have each other's back.

"You cold man?" Piccolo asked Jay. It wasn't his smoothest line ever, but then he wasn't trying to pick him up. Piccolo had always heard that if you didn't have anything to talk about then talking about the weather was always a good option – it gave you something that you were both feeling at that very moment, and it meant that you could quickly suss out their particular vibe. Besides, Piccolo had noted Jay's scarf and gloves and knew he was feeling the snap in the air. Winter was getting closer.

"I'm always cold nowadays," Jay answered. Piccolo turned a dial on the dashboard of the truck to crank the heating and moved the vent in his direction. "Thanks," Jay answered, a little hesitantly.

"You from somewhere warm originally?" Piccolo asked, concentrating on the road.

"No, not really." Jay said as he took off one of his gloves and put his palm against the vent. "I never used to really feel it, but now I feel like it's seeped into my bones or something. It's terrible, because it's not even winter yet. The temperature hasn't even really dropped much or anything, but I'm really feeling it."

"I like the cold," Piccolo told him. "Or at least, I like when it when it's still sunny and warm in the sunshine but there's a bit of a chill in the air. It makes it more pleasant to run in."

"You do a lot of running?" Jay asked. He was opening up a bit and asking questions, so Piccolo took it as a good sign.

"Yeah, I was on the track team. I won a scholarship to university because of running," Piccolo said. It wasn't in a boastful way, it was very matter-of-fact, but nonetheless he was proud of his accomplishments.

"Is that where you met the Professor?" Jay questioned.

"Yeah – he was my biomedical engineering professor. My parents told me if I wanted to run track at university then I had to take something else as well that was more in line with what they wanted for my future. They didn't believe in my dream of running professionally. They thought I needed a back-up option," Piccolo explained.

"Good parents do that," Jay said, slumping down into his seat. "At least they cared about you enough to take an interest. My parents didn't care at all."

"Did you go to university?" Piccolo asked, knowing the answer.

"Nah, I wasn't academic enough," Jay answered as Piccolo expected. "I couldn't be bothered really. I just wanted to play video games with my friend Danny."

Suddenly, Jay's face and mannerisms changed. He shut off completely and the conversation Piccolo had dragged out of him died. His face became a blank slate and his brown eyes dulled a little.

Piccolo knew instantly that he found the reason behind Jay's quiet state. He had found the one person he had lost that had meant the world to him.

"What happened to Danny?" Piccolo asked tentatively, looking sideways at Jay as he slowed down to round a tree-lined corner and start down the cobble path towards the Mt. Beryl Marina where Piccolo, Nora and Zeke had picked them all up.

"They did," Jay answered pointing out the front window of the truck.

Piccolo followed his finger and saw that they had arrived at their destination – the first of the ships that had landed near their home in the dirt car parking lot of the marina. The Visitor's ship was much larger up close and almost blocked out the view of the sky from their position on the road. Piccolo could make out the gas shimmering from the bottom of the metallic pipes that were sticking out of the ship, opened towards the earth. The ship had landed in the middle of the dirt road and had totalled it, creating a little nest of gravel, grass and dirt that it could sit in. Nearby, the tropical palm trees that had lined the grassy knoll had fallen to the ground and were smouldering from the impact.

There were several open holes in the middle of the ship and Piccolo could make out the Visitors scuttling around the landing site. They were monstrous and like nothing Piccolo had ever seen. They stood tall on large hind legs and their skin seemed to be made out of petrified muscle – all grey and ropey and clinging to a base of flesh underneath. Their large heads were in an oval shape that melded into a beak-like mouth and beady nostrils. Their eyes were a soulless black that Piccolo could see even from their distance up the road.

Piccolo was frozen in horror for a moment before Jay gave him a quick shove on the shoulder. Piccolo shook his head and flipped the truck's gears into reverse, using the mirrors to edge the truck backwards and then into an awkward three point turn just at the base of the road a little way away from where it cleared out into the parking lot. Jay fidgeted anxiously at the sound of the truck's heavy beeping and cocked his rifle. He leaned out of the passenger side door and took aim while Piccolo reversed the truck down past the turn, angling the back carriage of the truck towards the ship.

"They hear it – they're coming," Jay said. "It's now or never."

With that, Piccolo pumped the brake and put the truck into park. He quickly opened the driver's side door and jumped out, running towards the back of the truck. Jay used the passenger door to leverage himself up and onto the truck's roof.

Piccolo ran to the back of the truck, aware that several Visitors were scuttling up the dirt road towards him, alert to their presence and on the defensive. He breathed in quickly, fumbled with the metal latch at the truck's back door and letting his breath out, he unlocked the truck and pushed the sliding door towards the sky, opening it fully.

There Piccolo came face-to-face with a Mindless as it snarled in reaction to him. He let out a strangled yelp and jumped backwards as the Mindless reached for him, attempting to walk towards him and falling out of the truck. Piccolo dived forward and pulled the metallic lever on the other side of the door, releasing an automatic ramp at the back of the truck. The Mindless that had reached for him was struggling to get up from the ground before the ramp wedged itself and tore through the Mindless' torso.

It never made a sound as its body was severed and its entrails divided like the Red Sea against the automatic ramp. All it did was continue to reach for Piccolo as he took a step backwards and out of its reach.

By this time, countless Mindless were ambling down the ramp or falling off the side of the truck. They had been collected from various locations by Piccolo himself, and loaded into the trucks that the Professor had positioned close to the manor in the forest where they all lived. The Professor had been using these Mindless humans for experiments, trying to learn how the contamination had started and if there was a cure for the change. He had made amazing progress, but not to the extent that he had hoped. Instead, the Professor offered his walking cadavers as a distraction for the groups to seek out more of the Visitor's guns.

One or two of the Mindless closest to Piccolo started reaching for him, but the majority of the horde kept moving forward as they noticed the Visitors that were quickly approaching. The adrenaline in the Mindless started kicking in and their red irises flashed as they started to run to the Visitors.

Shots rang out above him, and Piccolo looked up to see Jay standing on the end of the truck with his rifle in his hands. His beanie had been blown off his head and his scarf blew in the wind as he took a cowboy-like stance on top of the roof. Piccolo saw his well-placed shot blast straight through one of the Visitors, who looked mildly irritated as a silvery mucus began to cover up the hole that the bullet wound had left.

It was at that moment that Piccolo really grasped what they were up against.

Jay shouted his name from the top of the truck and Piccolo looked back into the battlefield to find a blood-soaked Mindless right in from of him. Piccolo grabbed the Mindless by its bony shoulder in one hand and pushed it backwards away from him while drawing his own pistol up to its chin and firing off a shot. Dark blood and brain matter exploded from the back of the Mindless' head and it fell to the ground with a grunt.

Piccolo looked upwards and caught the tossed metallic cuff that Jay had commandeered from the Visitors in their previous battle. Piccolo had learnt how to use the space-aged weapon back at the manor before they had departed in the truck and he snapped the cuff on easily, pushing the buttons Victoria had shown him would release the gun. It worked, and in a series of metallic clinking sounds, a gun descended from a compartment on the cuff, shooting out in front of Piccolo's straightened wrist.

In a second the world seemed to slow as Piccolo took in the sight of the gun that had become an extension of him – but this was no time to marvel at the wonders of the universe. Piccolo shook himself out of his stupor and looked out onto the road.

The marauding Mindless from the truck had taken hold of the Visitors coming up the road, overpowering them with their greater numbers and sheer adrenaline. They took them down and ripped into their thick flesh. The Visitors that were overcome had started convulsing violently and Piccolo saw the unmistakable start of the transformation from the Mindless curse.

The Mindless feasting on the convulsing Visitors were attempting to eat them, but many were being shaken off by the convulsions. Several had already been faced with their final deaths as they had attempted to get to the Visitors, and were lying on the ground in a pool of blood and decay. Both sides were distracted and Piccolo saw his chance.

Aiming his wrist at the Visitors, Piccolo took a sharp breath in, held it and pressed one of the buttons that knew was the trigger for the weapon. A blinding flash of blue electricity buzzed out of the barrel of the gun and he was thrown back like he had been kicked by a mule.

The powerful blue electricity hit the backs and shoulders of several Mindless still trying to tear into one of the Visitors, but also hit the chin of the Mindless Visitor as it began to rise from its convulsion, changed. The Mindless and the Mindless Visitor imploded dramatically in their positions, congealing matter oozing from the orifices of both species. Piccolo let out a soft gasp as he watched greenish brain matter ooze from the beak, nostrils and soulless black eyes of the Mindless Visitor as they all slumped down onto the concrete of the road.

"Try not to get the Mindless, remember?" Jay called from the top of the truck. "We need them to change the Visitors!" Jay slung his rifle over his back and jumped over the opening at the back of the truck, landing with bended knees and a thud on the ground, his right gloved hand reaching out to steady himself. "Let's move them in closer!" he cried as he rose from his position off the ground.

Jay started running straight down the gravel road, pushing a Mindless out of his way but shouting at them to follow him. One of the other convulsing Visitors had started rising from a small horde of Mindless like a phoenix from the ashes, and looked towards Jay's flurry of motion with hungry eyes.

Piccolo saw the bright red iris that marked the contamination of the Mindless in its eyes as it watched Jay run, looking to spring into action. Piccolo pulled his arm around and aimed his wrist at the Mindless Visitor, pushing the button and setting the blue electricity off again. The red iris blinked before it disappeared into green ooze dribbling out of the Mindless Visitor's eyes as it imploded into itself.

A Mindless next to the Mindless Visitor fell as well, but the others all started running towards Jay, spurred into motion by their bloodlust. Piccolo saw four more Visitors running towards Jay from the ship, but he could also hear high-pitched screeches and gunshots from the ship as well.

The others had started their own simultaneous attacks using the Professor's horde of Mindless, and the ship was now being attacked on all sides.

Piccolo started running closer to the ship as well, shooting a couple of the Mindless in the head that neared him and trying not to think of the red congealed blood and brain matter oozing out of them as human brains. He ran to within a couple of feet of a convulsing Mindless Visitor on the road and shot its own species' weapon directly into its cranium. The proximity made it implode a little more dramatically than the others had, and Piccolo could feel his stomach churning and his own brain buzzing from the electric charge coming off the gun.

Piccolo then remembered why they were there, and he stopped to bend down and remove the cuff from the Mindless Visitor's body. A purple liquid had started pooling around the Mindless Visitor. Piccolo tried not to gag as he began to smell a noxious gas leaking out from the body. The cuff fell off the Mindless Visitor's wrist with a dull clang and Piccolo scooped it up and rose from his kneeling position.

Bodies lay everywhere around him on the road. Blood, bone, brain and entrails pooled over the concrete in a mix of dark reds and greens and purples. The three Mindless Visitors that had attacked them lay like grey heaps of mummified mass among the withered human bodies, and open mouths gaped at the sky. Piccolo felt his head swim as he took in the carnage – something so vivid that it was unlike any of the other attacks he had witnessed at the university.

He heard a yell from down the street and groggily Piccolo started in the direction of the spaceship. He saw the group of Mindless as they took down three of the Visitors on the side of the road, and more importantly Piccolo saw Jay standing at the side of the road, firing his rifle into two of the Visitors who had not yet turned and who were healing quickly with the shimmering mucus they excreted. Three of the Mindless hordes from the truck were closing in on his back as he tried to ward them off, but there were too many attackers and not enough space for Jay to move.

Piccolo started running. His legs pumped into action and his arms moved along his sides and he began the fastest sprint of his life. His heart pumped as he ran along the road, quickly bridging the gap between them.

But even Piccolo's fastest run wasn't fast enough.

It was a Mindless woman who did it. She was of medium height and build with frizzy brunette hair and freckles across her face. She wore a pair of dirty cheap jeans and a cheap flimsy green t-shirt that was so worn that it had started fading and rotting in areas. Her face had rat-like features, with stretched skin that shone with decay as she grabbed a hold of Jay with both hands and sank her teeth into his shoulder blade.

Jay let out a yell like a wounded bear as he pushed the butt of the rifle into the Mindless woman's head with all the strength he could muster. The Mindless woman was forced backwards as the butt entered her softened skull and broke through into the front of her brain, and letting go of Jay she fell to the concrete floor.

With the strength of its hind legs, a Visitor sprang at Jay and pushed him over on top of the Mindless woman's body, letting out a deafening roar like a lion before it attacked. But its roar turned into a shriek as other Mindless reached forward and grabbed at its shoulders. They tore into its gnarly flesh as it rose from Jay and tried to fend them off. Other Visitors had been set upon by the Mindless and a battle was waging.

Piccolo watched all of this happen as he sprinted as fast as he could towards Jay. Without thinking and without stopping, he raised his arm and fired the gun off towards the Mindless and the Visitors, who hadn't yet changed. The Mindless all fell into clumps of blood and decay, while the Visitors instead turned their attention to Piccolo as he ran nearer to them.

Piccolo watched as their black eyes lit up with a blue ringed iris before being changed through a darkened purple colour and into a red. They started stumbling on their strong legs and fell to the road.

"Jay! Jay!" Piccolo cried as he skidded to a stop and bent over Jay, adrenaline pumping in his veins and his breathing ragged.

Jay lay on the ground, half on top of the frizzy haired Mindless woman whose face was now battered in to an unrecognisable mash. He spat blood from his mouth as he tried to sit up.

"Don't move Jay!" Piccolo said, before he turned to each of the convulsing Mindless Visitors near them and fired the blue electricity into their heads. He turned and then one after another, fired the electricity into the human Mindless that were still trying to take down the Mindless Visitors. His own brain swam light-headedly from the constant electricity shooting from his wrist and the sprint he had just performed.

Jay didn't listen to him and rose to a seated position. Piccolo could see the bloody bite mark on his shoulder, pierced with the teeth of the Mindless. He had seen enough of the transformation to know that the contamination was probably already coursing through Jay's veins and making its way to his vital organs, destroying Jay's brain.

"I need to finish this ..." Jay said, his voice staggering a little.

"Let me do it Jay, I can get in and out of there in time," Piccolo told him, pushing against Jay's shoulder with his unarmed hand.

"There's no reason to put yourself in danger now," Jay answered him, coughing suddenly. "I've got the grenades and I know where to put them. I can make sure we end them now. Just start collecting the cuffs and get out of the way."

Piccolo nodded gravely, knowing what this meant. He had failed yet again. First Louise, and now Jay. He rose from his kneeling position and helped Jay to his feet, who stumbled a little and then cracked his neck to unstiffen his shoulders. He passed the rifle that was still in his hand to Piccolo. The butt was covered in blood, but he slung on his back without a thought.

"Tell them to end it," Jay said solemnly to Piccolo, looking him directly in his eyes. "Tell them to blow these mothers to kingdom come and off our planet. Tell Victoria to look after her baby, and tell Mia to stop worrying and that I love them, but I have a game I have to finish with Danny."

Piccolo nodded, and Jay put his arm on Piccolo's shoulder for a second that seemed to last for minutes before he looked pointedly at the watch he was wearing. The time read 2.25pm. Jay nodded and took off towards the ship, running at the fastest speed his damaged body could get to. Piccolo stifled a sudden urge to cry and set about doing what he needed to do – removing the cuffs from the bodies of the Mindless Visitors lying nearby. He pushed the button on his cuff that compacted the gun back into its compartment, stowed what he could in his pockets and snapped another cuff onto his other wrist. Piccolo looked up and saw Jay nearing the bottom of the ship. It was surprisingly clear of Visitors and Mindless but he could still make out the gun fire and the unmistakable sounds of the cuffs being fired from all around the ship. It seemed that they were winning.

But at how high a cost?

Piccolo realised he was still too close to the ship for Jay to set the explosions so started running back towards the truck and out of range. If this happened in the same way that they had calculated it would, he needed to be well away from the area. Piccolo heard Jay's shouts mixed with a other cries and he pumped his legs, sprinting to get closer to the truck.

He never looked back until he had reached the open back of the vehicle, then turned in just enough time to see Jay remove the two grenades that Valcheck had given him, from their clip on his jeans. He held one in each hand and made his way into a small hole that was open on the side of the ship, within climbing reach. Piccolo watched as Jay climbed deeper into the hole and disappeared from view.

Piccolo raised his wrist and looked at his own watch, straining against the leather band after it had been pushed higher up onto his forearm to make way for the Visitor's cuff. The watch showed 2.30pm – the time that the group had agreed everyone would need to be clear of the Visitors' ship.

A loud explosion ripped through the air and Piccolo raised his hand to shield his eyes. The grenades that Jay had been holding had finally exploded from inside the ship and the fire ripped through the otherworldly machine, mingling with the gas that propelled it into flight. The gas caught alight and secondary and tertiary explosions rocked the ship.

Flaming metal parts and thick Visitor body parts started raining down from the sky. A severed arm with suction cupped fingers landed with a sickening thud on the engine of the truck and the air from the blast pushed against Piccolo like a scorching wave. The truck's wheels started moving, pushed by the force of the blast of hot air, and Piccolo knew it was time to get out of there.

He turned on his heel and started to make a run for it up the dirt road where he and Jay had come from before he noticed Jay's grey beanie lying on the road in front of the truck. He remembered it being blown off Jay's head as Jay was standing on the truck's roof.

With only a moment's hesitation, Piccolo ran forward, stooped down and picked up the beanie in one smooth movement. With Hell breaking loose behind him, he sprinted up the road and prayed to God that everyone else was alright.

CHAPTER 7

Nora Dallas stood on the veranda of the house in the middle of the clearing, stooping lightly to protect the flame from her lighter as she lit the cigar that was wedged between her teeth. Once she felt the smooth smoke fill her lungs, she clicked off her lighter and straightened her back before she removed the cigar, holding the smoke tightly before breathing it out.

She was dressed as she had been when the group had descended upon the marina, in black jeans and chunky black boots, a black three-quarter sleeved shirt that hugged her slim body like a second skin, and her guns strapped to her thighs by a holster.

Nora and Zeke had followed Jay and Piccolo in the truck and had flanked the Visitors' spaceship centred in the Mt Beryl Marina car parking lot. They had approached on the other side of the tree line, hanging back while they watched Jay and Piccolo release the Mindless from the back of the truck. Once the Visitors were distracted, Nora and Zeke had attacked as well, stealing as many weaponised cuffs as possible. They had high-tailed it out of there before the bomb that obliterated the ship went off and hadn't figured out anything was amiss until they had returned to the manor.

Nora had pulled on a woven shawl over her combat outfit on her return and she hugged it into herself now, realising that she was painting a very contradictory picture of herself as she puffed on her cigar in her shawl.

But then again, Nora was more than happy to be seen as a contradiction.

Nora trained her luminous blue eyes across the house's yard and focused on the small group standing by the edge of the wall. It was made up of Victoria and Max Stone, Mia and Georgia Cavallari, and Piccolo Mein. Max had fashioned together a large cross of tree branches and twine and had placed it in the ground by the edge of the yard. They were using the cross as a marker to farewell their fallen friend Jay Welles, whose body had not returned from the mission.

In the heat of combat, they hadn't realised one of their comrades hadn't make it out – and had only heard the news from Piccolo when they returned to the house, They were weary from the battle that they waged on both ends of the nearby ship and most were devastated at the loss of Jay, but happy at having successfully retrieved more than thirty of the Visitors mysterious metallic cuffs. While Zeke had been more than willing to get straight into the thick of the battle, Nora had needed to steel herself when she first set eyes on the Visitors.

They seemed to her like creatures from a movie – an old science fiction one where Visitors from another planet came down to Earth and made an attempt to take over the world, only to be thwarted by an intelligent human with connections to either the government or the military. But this wasn't the type of movie she was accustomed to, and finding herself watching these strange creatures at close range – in real life, had initially terrified her.

Nonetheless, Nora had called on her strength and played her part against these Visitors, removing the metallic cuffs in the way that Victoria had shown them. She and Zeke had raced back through the thicket of the forest just as the explosion rocked through the air around them at exactly 2.30pm – the time that Jay was going to toss the explosions into the Visitors' ship.

Georgia's sister Mia had instantly broken down into tears on hearing the news of Jay when Piccolo finally returned to the manor clutching Jay's grey beanie. Mia had fallen to her knees in the middle of the back garden and Georgia bent down to hold her and they embraced tightly. Max and Victoria embraced each other with tears in their eyes when they heard the news.

Nora wasn't too concerned about the loss of Jay or even the effect it had on Piccolo, who had the pain etched all over his face. Everyone lost people, even before the outbreak began, and this wasn't a reason to give up.

It was a reason to make you stronger and more determined.

Nora's family had been dead to her long before the likelihood that they had actually died. She had grown up in a remote town that was miles away from the nearest city and her father had split on her and her mother when Nora was only ten months old. He had abandoned them for a life in the city and had come crawling back when Nora had made a name for herself. Luckily Nora had great lawyers who had been able to sweep the whole issue under the rug as quickly and as quietly as possible, but the sudden appearance of a man she had never known had been the only time that she had allowed herself to be emotionally shaken in her adult life.

Nora's mother had been left with very little of anything when her father took off, and she had taken up with several different men just to pay her bills. The kicker was when Nora was ten years old, her mother had married one of these men who turned out to be a drug dealer. He forced her mother to sell drugs with him, physically abused both of them, and when the police raided their home, her mother had taken the fall while the dealer ran off with another woman, never to be heard from again.

Suddenly, the helpless Nora was being passed around in the country from foster home to foster home until she ended up in the city. She never visited her mother in prison, and learnt quickly to be fast and strong and ready on her feet. She developed a thick skin against the multitude of bullies who tormented her in her foster homes and the few orphanages she ended up living in, and by the time she was fifteen years old she was a beautiful, intelligent and strong-willed women. She was determined to make sure that no one would ever hurt her again.

When she was shopping for five-finger discounts with one of her foster sisters she was approached by a woman who introduced herself as a talent agent. Gwen Staples had told Nora that she had what it took to be a model and that she should consider signing up with her. Nora's foster family had laughed at the idea and scoffed that there was no way in hell that the woman was legitimate, but Nora was determined to escape her hellish life so she signed up with the woman by forging her foster parents' signatures; the talent agency turned out to not only be legitimate, but actually very successful. Nora booked jobs across the city and started to see her star rise.

Unfortunately, her foster parents discovered her modelling success when she appeared on a TV advertisement, and the whole world had blown up around her. She was forced into legal counselling, her foster parents greedily took the money she had been saving, and Nora was devastated at seeing her fledgling career take such a dramatic turn so early on in her young life.

Nora begged Gwen for help and so she took over as Nora's foster mother and signed her up as a client to her business partner. Gwen had been the only woman in her life who had been like a real mother to Nora, and when she became ill with cancer when Nora was twenty-two, she, was determined to harden her heart to keep the pain at a distance. With Gwen's death she vowed no one else would ever penetrate her heart again.

As she matured, Nora kept her word, and didn't have many people that she trusted in her life. The only other person she had let in was her bodyguard Rohan. He was a bulky guy which gave him a presence despite his medium height. Nora regularly towered over him when she wore sky-high heels, but he was so solid and stocky that nothing seemed to bowl him over – physically or otherwise. Rohan had a sharp tongue that he wasn't afraid to use in an argumentative fashion, and he fought back with a slew of language so foul he could make grandmothers drop their walking sticks in shock.

Nora liked the fact Rohan was as surprising as she was. Under his tough demeanour, he was a passionate and charming man, with a wicked sense of humour that matched hers in intensity. He wasn't just her bodyguard, he was her friend, and she liked hanging out with him despite the fact that she paid him handsomely to do so.

Rohan had been with Nora on set the day of the outbreak. They were sitting on the sofa in her trailer drinking whiskey after a long day. Nora had been filming a tough fight scene and was dressed in her costume – a long black halter-necked pantsuit and chunky heels. Her make-up was perfectly done to portray her slightly grimy been-fighting-all-day-but-still-looks-good character, and her prop, a long-sabred katana, sat on the kitchen bench of the trailer.

Nora hated doing stunt fighting with the katana because it required getting up and close with people. She had done some training on how to use the weapon appropriately. The feudal sword was made only of a blunt steel, but still had a solid cut to it, which required concentration to ensure she didn't slice up her co-stars.

So as soon as the shots were cleared, Nora took herself back to her trailer for a stiff drink to take the edge of filming off. Rohan had met her in there and was now telling her all about his latest conquest – he was a bit of a womaniser who hated people getting too close, so whenever he felt too vulnerable he tended to ghost out. He had many women on regular rotation that seemed to get off on his tough demeanour yet soft heart, and like stray dogs, kept coming back for more.

Nora tended to trade war stories with Rohan – she was an emotional abuser of women just like he was.

"Oh my god she had the most perfect tits I have ever seen!" he laughed over his crystal tumbler. He was right in the middle of a story about a pretty brunette that he toyed with and kept her at a distance.

"And are you ever going to see those tits again?" Nora laughed wickedly and she took a sip of deep amber liquid. Rohan chuckled to himself as he set down his glass.

"God no. She wanted to *snuggle* afterwards. She put on my shirt and tried to make me spend the night. No way am I seeing that clingy bitch again!" he answered.

Nora and Rohan burst into laughter, but as it peeled back into a chuckle they were momentarily hushed by a blood-curdling scream from outside the trailer. They both looked up from the plush sofa, locking eyes momentarily.

"What the hell was that?" Nora asked, setting down her crystal tumbler and rising from the couch. Rohan went straight into bodyguard mode and shot right up to his full height. He moved towards the venetian blinds that had been drawn across the side of the trailer and with a flick of his deft fingers split the blades. He moved his eyes closer and peered out into the lot around the trailer.

"What is it Rohan?" Nora asked again, her eyes widening.

Suddenly Rohan jumped back from the window, instantly closing the slit between the venetian blinds. Just as he jumped backwards, Nora felt a sick thud against the side of the trailer wall, right where he had been standing. Again and again, she felt dull thuds reverberate through the trailer like someone was banging on the sides of the walls. Nora had felt something similar a couple of times before, as fans thudded on the windows of her limousine as they pulled away from an event or two, but this felt different.

This felt violent.

"Rohan!" Nora's voice rose over the dull thuds. "Rohan, what is it?" Nora stalked forward towards the side of the trailer that the banging was coming from and pulled the cord to the venetian blinds, opening them to the world.

"Don't …" Nora heard Rohan say behind her as he reached out to stop her, but it was too late.

Outside the trailer was pure carnage. There were people everywhere, but not in the usual way a studio back lot was busy. Nora watched in horror as people were running and screaming in all directions, some falling down onto the hard cement below them. There were people she recognised from the studio wearing jeans and sneakers and blazers running after others. As they reached for them, they pulled their co-workers down like a hungry cheetah would take down a gazelle. They jumped and dived on top of them, smashing their heads into the concrete, spraying the lot with bursts of blood.

Nora watched in horror as her make-up artist with bright pink hair sank her teeth into the ear of a runner and pulled, tearing the thin tissue off in one go. Blood spurted onto the concrete in an arterial display as the make-up artist hungrily chewed into the flesh that had only a moment ago been attached to the runner's head.

As Nora's eyes danced around the hellish scene her attention was pulled towards an immediate danger as a hand smashed against the window that she had pulled open. The forced rattled the thin glass and a brownish red smear followed the hand as it slid down the window. Next to the hand was the face of her co-star who had retreated into the trailer that was situated next to hers after their previous scene together. He was a handsome man, with stylishly combed blonde hair and a mega-watt smile, but his brilliant chocolate brown eyes were staring at her hungrily through the glass – and not in the way he had previously stared at her ass when they had first met.

His eyes were rimmed with red and they glinted like a devils wings in the sunlight outside. There was blood all around his mouth and a gaping bite wound in his neck. Through the trailer window Nora could see deep into the wound and saw it was a tangle of blood, muscle and flesh.

Nora was absolutely stunned. Suddenly her stock standard action movie had become a real-life slasher film. Surely it had to be some sort of joke? Her make-up artist hadn't really just torn off someone's ear – surely it was all special effects?

But something deep inside Nora knew that the gore was real.

Her co-star raised his hand again and smashed it against the glass, this time shattering the window. His hand raked through the air as he reached inside, shards rained down around him and embedded into his skin. Nora could now hear the moans and the screams of the outside back lot clearly through the smashed window.

Suddenly, Rohan's arms encircled Nora's slender waist and pulled her backwards. "We have to go – now!" he cried into her ear, and pulled her towards the trailer's front door. As they approached the door, Rohan scrambled for the katana lying on the bench in the kitchen. It was a stunt weapon, but it would have to do.

Rohan stopped at the door and peered through the porthole window. He put up three fingers in Nora's direction and then lowered them one by one, counting down. Rohan pulled his right leg back and kicked straight above the doorknob, shattering the lock and blowing the door open with the pressure. As he did, a few studio workers who had been trying to get inside the trailer were pushed backwards and Rohan stepped out into the back lot, alert to the danger that was all around them.

Nora stepped down the stairs of the trailer and out behind him as Rohan reached and put a protective arm across her body. They sidled away along the trailer to the front and looked around the corner of the large metallic caravan.

The carnage was just as terrifying outside the trailer as it had been viewed from the inside. Screams filled the air and there was a strong smell of iron and other foul-smelling human secretions. The make-up artist with the pink hair rounded the trailer next to them with a loud groan and Nora jumped back in fear as she took in the pink hair that was now mixed with bright red blood and had bits of human flesh dangling in it.

The make-up artist reached out for Nora with her blood-covered hands and Rohan wasted no time in raising the katana above his head and bringing it down. Despite the bluntness of the sword, the steel sliced directly through the outreached hands of the make-up artist, and her detached hands landed with a sickening thud on the concrete below. Blood sprayed out of the stubs left behind and splattered all over Rohan's dark duffle coat and Nora's black halter pantsuit.

The make-up artist let out a sickening roar and kept motioning towards them, her bloody stumps still squirting and reaching for them with phantom limbs. The bones glistened white against the sun and blood inside the stumps. Stunned momentarily at the fact that he had just sliced a woman's hands off, Rohan paused just long enough for the make-up artist to reach for Nora – the bloody stumps closing in towards her face.

Nora reacted and grabbed the woman's elbows, which were slick with blood. She attempted to shove the bloody and leaking stumps away from her face, pushing with all her might, only letting go as she felt the make-up artist move backwards with gravity. The woman's chunky heeled boots stepped onto one of her own hands lying on the ground, which was so slick with blood that she slipped and crashed to the ground. Without anything to break her fall, her head cracked loudly onto the concrete, bouncing slightly. Her red rimmed irises flashed momentarily as blood began to pool around her head like a halo. Her eyes remained open to the scene above them as she lay there.

Nora could feel panic starting to bubble up from deep within her, as her mind took in the scene. The make-up artist certainly looked pretty dead – deader than she had a minute ago when she had attacked them.

"Oh my god, oh my god, oh my god!" Nora started muttering, holding her hands out in front of her, clawed, slightly shaking and covered in blood. A loud series of groans could be heard getting closer behind them.

Rohan seemed to have recovered faster than she had, because suddenly he was grabbing Nora's blood soaked hands with one of his own meaty paws.

"Nora, c'mon, we have to go," Rohan told her and tugged her around the front of the trailer, avoiding the body of the fallen make-up artist. As Nora stepped gingerly past the puddle of blood that had pooled out from the body and followed him, Rohan pointed to the large cement wall of the studio to the right of the trailers.

"Let's head towards the gate and find a car. Stay as close as you can to the wall," Rohan told her. Nora nodded gravely, and suddenly he took off in front of her, katana at the ready. Nora followed, aiming for the wall and training all her thoughts on getting there while Rohan ran a little to the left of her, shielding her way from the rest of the back lot. Nora hit the wall with her outstretched and bloody fingers, and felt the cool of the plaster through her slick fingertips. She turned to look for Rohan and was shocked by what she saw.

He had raised the katana in front of him and wasted no time in slashing the sword into Nora's co-workers on the set. He sliced through limbs, sending arterial blood splatters everywhere and he slashed at them, one after another, with a terrifying velocity.

A studio executive in jeans and sneakers ran with his arms outstretched towards him, and without even a moments' consideration, Rohan lodged the katana straight into the executive's stomach, all the way to the hilt. The long steel of the tip of the blade was visible through the studio executive's back.

Rohan let out a blood-curdling scream into the executives face as he did so, running on adrenaline and rage. The executive let out a gurgling scream that was mixed with blood as it spurted out of his mouth. It was then that Rohan took in the executive's eyes – a normal hazel brown colour without a shred of glowing red in them; he realised that the executive wasn't an attacker like the rest of them – he wasn't one of the Mindless humans who had turned on the others.

The executive was innocent, and had only been trying to get away. He had seen Rohan in defensive mode, and had run to him for protection.

With all his might, Rohan pulled the katana out of the man and a sheath of blood followed the steel, splattering Rohan's coat further. The studio executive looked down and grasped at his gaping and bleeding wound before he fell to the ground as well, moving his gaze up to stare at Rohan in finality.

Rohan breathed heavily from where he was standing, and all he could do was watch as the dark-skinned caterer in a checked shirt approached the man and knelt down, aiming his bloody mouth into the studio executive's voice box, ripping it out in one go.

Suddenly, Nora was grabbed at the shoulder by her co-star who had broken the window of her trailer, his red-rimmed eyes still flashing in hunger towards her. Nora let out a startled scream which shocked Rohan from his stupefied stance, and he started towards her.

As the co-star grabbed at the flesh on her shoulder, Nora clenched her right fist and aimed it directly at the co-star's pretty-boy face. She clocked him straight in the nose and she could both feel and hear the small nose bones breaking and splintering under her fist. The co-star was sent reeling momentarily before the thing he had become righted itself and looked at her with anger raging inside him. Nora could see cartilage peeking out from the bridge of his nose – no longer handsome, he was quite a revolting sight with his red-rimmed eyes, the blood dripping from his mouth and destroyed nose.

As a snarl began to escape from his lips, Nora watched in horror as Rohan neared the co-star from behind, raised the katana and sliced it directly through her co-star's neck. It sliced through the muscle, flesh and bone with only a slight push back, and as the blade finished its trajectory, droplets of blood came out with the steel. The co-star's snarl continued as his head began to slide from its position on the top of his neck and landed with a thick dull thud on the concrete of the back lot.

His body stayed stock still for a second, and Nora could only look in wide-eyed horror past the bloody stump of the neck over at Rohan standing behind him. The body then followed suit and sagged to the floor, banging its shoulder on the ground. Blood beginning to pool from the gaping neck, mixing with the tangle of flesh that was already escaping from the base of the head.

"Keep going!" Rohan cried at Nora and grabbed her left shoulder, which was beginning to bruise from the co-stars grasp, pushing Nora backwards to face the exit before they continued to take off towards the gate. Their run towards the studio's boom gate was primarily unmolested, and they left a huge chunk of the action behind.

As Nora raced around the edge of the boom gate she saw the face of the security guard pressed against the window of the secure box he sat in. His eyes were wide in terror with his face half turned towards the boom gate she was now rushing behind. A man with an out-dated salt and pepper haircut with round-rimmed glasses was half hanging out of the door of the box, feasting on the security guard. The man in a mindless daze, with red rings reflecting through his round spectacles, was tearing pieces off the security guard's face like strips of tissue paper, devouring each slice while the security guard moved his mouth in wordless pain, reaching against the glass.

Rohan approached the boom gate with a running jump and leapt completely over the striped painted guardrail. He landed with a hard thud on his boots and he kept running towards the parking lot of the studio.

"Rohan!" Nora cried, unable to turn away from the horror in the secure box. Rohan stopped in his tracks and turned to her, motioning for her to keep following him.

"Please, Rohan. Help him!" Nora cried, pointing to the security guard being devoured alive.

"He's done for Nora, keep going." Rohan cried, turning his back on her and making towards the cars again. Nora could barely believe what he was doing.

"Rohan!" Nora screamed again, letting out a high-pitched wail that she used to her advantage when she'd needed to be a diva. The loud scream alerted the Mindless around her to her presence and the bespectacled man in the secure box dropped a slice of the security guard's cheek to gnash its teeth towards her instead.

The scream made Rohan stop in his tracks, grunting angrily. He turned around and ran back towards Nora with a deafening roar, moving the katana into slicing position as he picked up speed. The bespectacled man had moved out of the secure box and rounded the corner to reach for Nora, who stayed where she was with Rohan approaching. As Rohan reached them, he sliced the katana through the air and with all of his might he forced the edge of the blade into the neck of the salt and pepper-haired man.

The blunt katana lodged itself in the middle of the man's throat and was finally caught, the back of his neck spurting blood and a wet choking sound coming out of his mouth. The man still reached for Nora despite the damage done to his neck and as he made to grab her, Nora instead took a hold of his broad shoulders and pushed backwards, sending his body back but leaving his half severed head moving forward. The extra pressure dislodged the katana from where it was stuck in his sinew and the head sliced off in one smooth movement.

The half-head of the man with the salt and pepper hair fell forward and landed in Nora's hands, bits of flesh dangling off the ends and his glasses askew. Nora instantly dropped the head in horror and it landed with a wet thud on the cement.

Rohan bent down to pick up the katana that had been dislodged and he stared in annoyance at the fact that the blunt stunt blade had finally snapped in two. He grunted angrily and looked up at Nora with half-closed eyes of annoyance.

"We'd still have a weapon if you didn't want to save this guy Nora," Rohan harshly chastised her. He dropped the top half of the blade and it clattered with a steely sound before he stopped and put his hands in the pockets of the salt and pepper-haired man's pants. Rohan pulled out a set of keys with a dice keyring attached.

Apparently this guy hadn't left the glorious times of the eighties.

Rohan walked around to the secure booth and drove the broken end of the katana through the soft missing cheek muscle of the security guard, whose now red-rimmed eyes flickered as the broken steel met his brain. Rohan pulled the broken sword out again and then dropped it on the ground next to him in a show of defiance.

Loud moans and screams started coming up closely behind them and Rohan headed towards the cars again, clicking the unlock button of the eighties-style key fob into the air until the salt and pepper-haired man's shiny black car lights flashed in response. Nora took off behind him and they jumped into the sleek black sedan. Rohan jumped behind the wheel, shoved the key into the ignition and pulled the hand break off in one swift motion, before he peeled out of the lot. Nora could feel the thuds at the back of the car as he drove over two of the Mindless studio workers who had been chasing after them.

Nora and Rohan headed out of town in the black sedan, barely saying anything to each other as they watched the world around them burn. Nora watched the streets race by them and was faced with even more horrific images than what she had just witnessed at the studio. Several times Rohan had to drive around bodies lying in the middle of the road, being devoured steadily in a bloody frenzy by other human beings.

Nora hadn't said anything to Rohan and he hadn't said anything to her, but she knew that he was taking it in and trying to process what he had done – all the killing, the beheading, and even of people who had only been asking for his help. Rohan had always been self-serving and had a tenacious love for the more violent side of life, but she knew his vulnerable side must have been waging war inside him.

Still, if a hurricane was blowing inside his mind, Nora would never know about it under his smooth dark-skinned poker face.

They ran out of gas outside of the town, about four hours down the road from the oblivion they had witnessed and left behind. They had been heading east and were on an empty unused road covered in trees and tall grass when the car sputtered its last breath, finally out of gas. Rohan swore loudly behind the steering wheel and they both got out of the car.

"What do we do now?" Nora asked, putting a hand above her eyes to shield them from the afternoon sun as they walked around the car.

"It looks like we're walking. We might be able to find a house or something along the road if we keep going, but there's no other way we can get there without gas," Rohan answered. He pulled a cigarette out of the packet he kept in the breast of his now blood-splattered duffle coat, putting it to his lips.

"The sun is going to set soon – shouldn't we just stay here and spend the night in the car and then head off in the morning?" Nora suggested. Rohan stooped to light his cigarette, his hunched shoulder dismissive of Nora's suggestion and focused on lighting his poison.

Suddenly, Rohan and Nora were alerted to the presence of a Mindless human as it walked out from the tree line close to them. She wore a long blue ruffled dress and had long straight blonde hair, and other than the deadened look in her red-rimmed eyes and the large blood stain that ran down her shoulders and dress she would be able to pass for a normal human. She stopped at the sight of them, and her groan became louder as the adrenaline of seeing fresh meat began to course through her veins.

Behind her, more Mindless began to appear from the tree line. There were men and women, children and teenagers all in various states of decay and gore. Crimson blood was splattered all over them, skin was scraped off knees and arms, some were even missing an arm or two – white bone protruding into the evening sunlight. Bites were visible all over the flesh of the Mindless and flies buzzed around their evisceration and gaping wounds.

Each one of them had bright red-rimmed irises and each of these irises flashed in hunger in their direction.

Rohan let out a curse and dropped his burning cigarette to the ground. The moans became louder as they backed towards the car. Rohan reached into the car to find a weapon and forgot that the katana had broken back at the studio. He let out another curse and straightened up, thinking fast.

"What do we do Rohan?" Nora asked, taking in the large group of Mindless that had begun snarling at them.

"Move to the boot!" Rohan instructed her, and pushed her down the edge of the sedan to the car's shiny boot. He popped the release from under the wheel of the driver's side and the trunk bonnet swung upwards. Quickly, Rohan raced to the back of the car, leaving the driver's side door open, and reached in, pulling the bottom panel of the car's trunk out. He clasped his hands around the tyre iron and pulled the bar out of spare tyre compartment.

"Get in Nora!" Rohan instructed, and she looked at him in horror.

"I can't! What are you going to do?" Nora exclaimed.

"There's no time Nora. I can fight them off but I need you to get in the trunk. I'm going to close it on you and they won't be able to get to you and I will let you out when I can," he told her.

The Mindless girl in the blue dress made a run for them, and Rohan anticipated her move. He readied himself and swung the tyre iron at her, catching her square in the eye with the heavy metallic gear at the end. It made a sickening sound of metal on skin, and the Mindless girl fell to the ground, her eye socket caved in and bloody.

"I. Will. Let. You. Out." Rohan shouted at Nora. "Get in!"

Nora did what he said, climbing into the trunk of the car. She grabbed the lip of the bonnet and pulled and the last thing she saw was Rohan readying himself as the Mindless horde began to move in.

Inside the dark and cramped trunk Nora heard everything. She heard every guttural reaction from both Rohan and the Mindless. She heard every swing and every crunch of metal into bone and flesh. She heard every blood splatter and every crunch of the gravel beneath their feet. But she never heard Rohan fall. He had moved the fight away from the car for her protection, but after what seemed like hours the outside world was finally silent.

And Nora waited.

She heard the sound of crickets as the night rolled in, but during that first night of being alone that was all she heard. She heard footsteps shuffle past at one point, but she recognised it instantly as someone who moved without direction or purpose.

She recognised it as the sound of the Mindless searching for their next meal.

The hunger pains kicked in, as did the need for water. Her tongue was practically sandpaper at this point and she kept licking her lips to moisten them. She had searched every inch of the dark boot to find a way out but she found nothing – no clasp, no secret compartment, and no light. Her need to go to the bathroom subsided as her thirst took over.

And still she waited for Rohan to let her out.

Eventually, Nora fell asleep.

A cramp in her arm woke her up with a start and she began to panic. Her breathing was short and ragged and she struggled to comprehend her surroundings. She had no idea how long she had been asleep, or what time it was, or why Rohan had never returned for her. She began to sob in deep breaths and then struggled to stop when she realised she was using up her oxygen faster, putting herself in more danger. She tried to slow her breathing, but it was ragged and hard.

Where was Rohan? Why hadn't he come back? Had he lost the battle with the Mindless out there?

Soon after she had managed to slow her breathing down, Nora heard a sound. It was the crunch of the gravel under heavy duty boots, but it was a purposeful step; quiet, resourceful, but present. This was not the gait of a Mindless, who shuffled aimlessly.

Nora knew it was her chance to escape. She licked her lips and started banging on the roof of the trunk. She screamed Rohan's name over and over again, using her training in vocal projection to will her voice through the metal of the car.

Suddenly the trunk swung open above her and Nora blinked into the brilliant sunlight, trying to cover her face.

"Rohan?" she practically sobbed. She strained against the blinding sun and all she saw was the outline of a stocky muscular figure above her.

"I don't know who Rohan is but he's not here," said a voice with a thick Russian accent. The man reached into the boot and took Nora's hand and she allowed him to pull her up. She shivered in the sudden warmth of the sun and struggled to see correctly against the blinding light of day. The Russian put a bottle to her lips and her tongue could instantly feel the cool refreshing drink of water. She grabbed the bottle from him and chugged greedily.

"How long have you been in there?" The Russian asked.

Nora finished chugging and set the cantina back in his hand. "I don't know," she said. "Where's Rohan? Who are you?"

"I take it Rohan locked you in the boot and fought his way out," the man said, indicating the piles of dead bodies that were strewn around the boot of the car. They lay heaped in blood that had dried in the sun, but was still relatively fresh. Nora guessed she might have been in there for the night and the morning.

Nora scanned the dead bodies, which continued to be strewn up the road, but she couldn't make out Rohan's duffle coat or dark skin. He was nowhere among the deceased.

Which meant he had either abandoned her, or had been turned and had shuffled away with the rest of the Mindless.

Nora looked back at the man, who had slicked-back black hair and a neat black goatee. He wore a black leather jacket and had a kind face.

"I'm Valcheck," he told her as he reached out his hand to her. "This is Georgia and Zeke," he pointed to two people standing on the other side of the road with rifles in their hands at the ready. It was the first time Nora had seen them behind the harsh glow of the sun.

"Who is this Rohan? Do you know where he's gone? Do you know where you're going?"

Nora shook her head in disbelief. She just couldn't imagine Rohan leaving without her.

Or would he? How much did she really know her friend? In an end-of-the-world crisis – which it definitely seemed like it was – her money was no good to him and she had proved by wanting to save that man at the security guard desk that they had different intentions in mind.

"What is your name?" Valcheck asked again, cupping her elbow with his meaty hand as she started to shake.

"I'm Nora," she told him as she began to hug herself despite the warmth of the sun. She was so torn and so confused.

"Well it's lovely to meet you Nora," Valcheck told her in his thick accent. "Nora, would you like to come with us? We have food and water and weapons, and we can help you. We can help you find Rohan if you would like?"

Nora looked into Valcheck's eyes and saw no trace nor hint of red-rimmed irises. He had a tough but kind demeanour and she trusted him instantly. Nora nodded and Valcheck nodded in return. At that point, Georgia the slim brunette on the road, approached and took the dark brown hoodie off her back, slinging it onto Nora's bare shoulders. Nora hugged it closely to her thin frame and dutifully followed after them.

A lot had changed for Nora since that day. She was no longer the princess locked in an ivory tower who needed bodyguards and protection. She had already been trained in martial arts for her many roles in action movies but Georgia, Valcheck and Zeke had helped her to hone those skills, and to maximise her own strength against the Mindless. Other than that first day when she had appeared weak and clinging on to the hope of seeing Rohan again, Nora had vowed never to mention him. It was embarrassing to think he had possibly left her in the boot of a car to rot.

But then again, he could have been rotting somewhere himself, and here she was hating him for it. It was a strange sort of kismet.

Finding Rohan was part of the reason that Nora was keen to be a scout for the group. She always had her ears to the ground and her eyes on every Mindless that scuttled by —always looking. It wasn't that she wanted to team up and be a motley crew again, or even to get revenge on his abandoning her.

It was the unanswered question of where he went and what happened to him that burned in her brain, and she was restless without the answer.

Nora sucked in the smooth smoke of her cigar as she thought of Rohan coolly sucking on his own cigarettes. Her therapist would have told her that her never-ending search to find Rohan was probably some sort of deluded result of never really knowing her father and for being abandoned by both him and her mother.

Her therapist was right about that. She definitely had abandonment issues.

It seemed impossible to love someone but hate someone so much. To spend so much time trying not to think of them but wondering where they went and what compelled them to do what they did. It was the unpredictable nature of humanity and it was why she almost preferred the company of the Mindless; the senselessness of it all had a reason.

For there was no reason in the end.

The memorial of Jay Welles was coming to an end, but Piccolo was approaching her after leaving the last words to the friends who had been with Jay from the beginning. Nora could read the sorrow on his face like an open book – she had been forced to emulate it during her career after all.

"There was nothing you could do," Nora said as Piccolo approached the porch. She let out the smoke that she had been holding in her lungs. "We're in the middle of two wars and we weren't even aware that we were fighting one of them until these guys showed up," Nora spat bitterly before she turned to Piccolo and looked at him with slightly softened eyes. "It's better him than you."

Piccolo stopped and looked at Nora hard with his hurt eyes. "How can you say that? How can you just be OK with the idea of people dying around you and think, 'well, at least it wasn't me'".

"Because everybody dies Piccolo. Whether they die here and now or die later, we're all going to die. You didn't die today, so you get to do something about it tomorrow. Jay did. At least he's not walking around, alone and decayed." Nora jerked her head towards the outside world, indicating that at least he wasn't a Mindless. "At least he did something with the end of his life by blowing up that ship. It's more than a lot of people can say."

A throat clearing behind them made Piccolo jump, but Nora was used to it. She casually turned back towards Valcheck who was standing by the door behind her. He was always sneaking up on her – it was like a game they played. Her cigar was almost finished and damned if she was going to let that pregnant Victoria put it out.

"You're right Nora," Valcheck told her, "Jay died a hero. He helped us get our hands on many of the Visitor's cuffs and took down a ship all on his own. There's none of us here who can say that." Nora blew the smoke in Valcheck's direction. He knew what she was getting at – he was the only one she had trusted enough to let know.

Valcheck pretended not to notice as he approached Nora and with surprisingly deft fingers, took the remains of her cigar and puffed on it himself. He took a long, heavy drag and then butted the remains on the wood of the porch.

"We need more Mindless," he said. "We need them gathered in the second smaller truck. Any volunteers?"

"I'll go," Nora said straightening her spine. "Give me Zeke. We'll get you what you need."

"I know you will," Valcheck answered as he let out the smoke. He turned on his heel and walked back inside the well-lit house, leaving Nora and Piccolo standing where they were.

Nora knew exactly what they needed to win the war, but what she really needed was answers. They were out there – somewhere. She just needed to get her hands on them.

CHAPTER 8

Once Professor Buddy Malone got his hands on the Visitors' cuffs that the group had collected he disappeared into the laboratory with the still distraught Piccolo, and worked tirelessly to study the engineering of the weapons. The testing and the creation of the bombs would take some time and Georgia worried that time was not on their side, especially with the destruction of one of the Visitors' ships. With every rustle in the bushes, the group deployed their remaining cuff guns, forever unsure if they would meet a dirty and bloodthirsty Mindless, or a sleek and calculating Visitor out for revenge.

They could hear the grinding of machinery and the sound of explosions as more ships of the Visitors settled in. Unsure of what to do, the group split into squads to continue their duties: Nora and Zeke rounded up Mindless and prepared the necessary requirements for the battle ahead of them, while Max and Valcheck went on scouting missions to watch the Visitors, making sure they weren't going to get anywhere near their encampment and ruin the surprise the group had in store for them.

That meant that while Piccolo and Professor Malone worked in the lab, Victoria and Georgia were the lookouts at the house.

Victoria hated being left behind, and was quite vocal about being split up from her husband, but her pregnancy meant that it was safer for her to remain at the house. She still had not told Max about the wave of Visitor-like morning sickness that had overcome her that day on the beach at the marina and she had felt guilty about that, but the feeling had not emerged again.

In fact, her human morning sickness seemed to have eased as well. It was not as she expected though, and Victoria worried incessantly about the child in her womb. She purposely stayed away from the Professor and his lab, trying to ease herself into a slightly more relaxing mental and physical environment. His work on the Visitors' cuffs made her think of the time long ago when the military were testing nuclear bombs and the subsequent effects of radiation. Because of this fear, Victoria spent more time out of the house on patrol to avoid anything that could potentially harm the baby.

She had even removed the precious cuff that she had worn on her wrist since the first attack, a motion that had not gone unnoticed by the rest of the group.

Georgia found the whole idea ridiculous, as Victoria had already been exposed to the Visitors and their guns. She had been quick to point out that any radiation being emitted from the weaponised cuff would have already been absorbed by her foetus and there was no telling what kind of damage would be emitted just by having the Visitors in such close proximity to them. Victoria had outwardly dismissed Georgia's claims, but had been unnerved at how easily Georgia had been able to read her fears.

However, it wasn't the only judgement Georgia made on Victoria. She couldn't fathom the idea of having a child in a world plagued by the Mindless, let alone the Mindless and the Visitors. It seemed irresponsible.

But Georgia had always been wary of children, even when her sister Joan had brought home Georgia's little niece and nephew. Georgia found that children were just a bundle of responsibility that she didn't want. She lived for herself and preferred it that way.

Until she had lost Mia.

Mia had been her annoying kid sister – eager to please and wanting to be just like her. Georgia had been forced to take care of Mia and Joan when their parents went out and it annoyed her as it would any eldest child. But as she ran past her dying father into the woods that fateful day, Georgia realised she desperately wanted nothing other than to find Mia and pull her close.

She had lost her whole family in one awful day and so had ended up with what she had always wanted – to be alone.

So she did what she always did; the only thing she could do in an act of desperation. She took care of herself. She chose to save the only life she could save at that moment in time, and she saved it by joining Valcheck.

Since then Georgia had fallen completely in love with Valcheck Stoll. Georgia was a strong, stubborn and resilient woman, but she let him in fully and he loved her in return. He was stoic and thoughtful, but he listened and he understood, and more importantly he cared. He never told her she was wrong, even when deep down she knew that she always had been.

But in a world gone cold and dark, and despite being in love – or perhaps because of it, Georgia realised that she hadn't wanted to be alone at all. She searched desperately for Mia, and when the group came up the road with Mia, she clung to the hope of never being alone again.

Georgia felt like she had to make it right. She had found Mia only by the grace of the group, and she had to thank them for that. Because of that, Georgia pushed aside her questioning of

Victoria's decisions, mindful that her own had led to years of guilt and remorse, and went to find the co-leader of the new group.

Victoria was standing near the fence at the end of the property near the body-less grave that had been marked for Jay. Her rifle was resting in both hands at the ready, but Georgia could see her mind was wandering.

"Do you mind if I join you?" Georgia asked softly, making Victoria jump slightly. She breathed out sharply and turned to find Georgia approaching. Victoria blinked a couple of times, obviously having been lost in thought.

"I'm sorry. I guess I wasn't being a very good sentry," Victoria answered.

"No, it's not that at all." Georgia replied, walking up and standing next to her. "I realised I haven't thanked you for bringing Mia home to me; for taking care of her, and I'm sorry I haven't acknowledged that yet."

Victoria smiled, "It was an absolute no brainer. She said you used to live in that apartment block, right? She was searching for you too. It was hope that brought her to us – the hope to find you again and that same hope brought her here. Hope is the most important thing that you can have in a world such as this."

"I'm ashamed to say that I didn't have hope," Georgia answered, hanging her head slightly as her brunette hair fell into her eyes. "I searched, but I couldn't find her, and when confronted with the idea that she might never be found I chose to take the easy way out rather than to keep looking. I abandoned her. I can never forgive myself for that."

Georgia continued, desperate for acceptance and approval from this woman who in every way had saved her sister and delivered her from death – a job that should have been Georgia's.

"Growing up it was very typical of me. I was selfish. I abandoned my family and the farm and moved to the city –

eager to make a name for myself that was better than what they had provided for me. When the horde hit us I abandoned them to die in that farmhouse; I abandoned my father as he was feasted on in the woods. And then I met Valcheck and I abandoned my search for Mia. I've been trying to make up for this ever since. So really, I need to thank you. You did more for Mia than I ever did."

With that, Georgia held out her hand for Victoria to take, who looked into Georgia's eyes and she took the hand into a handshake.

"Mia loves you Georgia," Victoria told her. "You are family and it is unconditional. She never considered that you abandoned her for a minute. This dreadful new world has abandoned us all but it is only with strength and hope for the future that we have not abandoned it."

"Is that why you are going through with having the baby?" asked Georgia hesitantly, "if you don't mind me asking?" She was desperate to understand.

Victoria dropped her hand from Georgia's and put it back on the butt of the rifle. She looked out past the forest.

"I am having this baby because this world needs a future. We can't let the Visitors take it, and we can't let the Mindless claim it. We fought and evolved and grew to be a part of this world, and while the human race did its best to destroy it in a hedonistic search for development, the beauty of the world is still here. It deserves to be protected and for whatever reason we are the ones who are left to do the protecting … all of us. We didn't make it this far not to."

Victoria looked back at Georgia as she nodded in understanding. "I also love Max with all of my heart. Our plan was always to have children before all of this happened, so to be finally blessed with a child and not heed the call would be so detrimental to the love and hard work we put into our relationship. I hope for the best, always, and I know that the idea of having an unpredictable hazard screaming an alert to the Mindless is not ideal, but nothing in this world is ideal right now. We work with the hands we are dealt."

"I don't agree with your decision to have a child," Georgia told her, "but I understand the love you have is stronger than anything else. I never wanted children, but I know that I love Valcheck and if we were to fall pregnant I don't know if I could give that up."

"It becomes a part of yourself. It's you and your love together in unity. That's a hard thing to give up," Victoria answered.

Suddenly, their attention was drawn away from the conversation and brought in to a rustle in the trees as something approached. Victoria raised her rifle and crouched, taking aim at the trees while Georgia pulled her pistol from her holster, aiming it in the same direction.

"It's just us!" Max called as he and Valcheck emerged from the trees, one hand in the air and one still on their weapons. Instantly, Victoria and Georgia dropped their sights and scrambled over to meet them as they let themselves in through the gate's entrance.

As Victoria rushed into Max's arms, Georgia felt overcome with emotion and hurried to plant a long hard kiss on Valcheck, holding his face to hers with both hands. Valcheck was caught slightly off guard by Georgia's sudden passion but he settled into it, reaching down with his hand and cradling her lower back, his weapon hand relaxed by his other side.

After what felt like hours, Valcheck pulled away from Georgia's embrace and raised a dark eyebrow at her. A shadow of a smirk ran over his lined face as he grinned down at her.

"What? Did you miss me babe?" he chuckled as he playfully slapped her butt. Georgia giggled slightly at the impact before she realised that Victoria and Max were watching them and regained her composure.

"How did the scout go?" Georgia asked, clearing her throat before she began speaking.

"Good," Max answered, his arms still around Victoria's own thickening waist. "They are still some way off from us and we didn't encounter them getting closer. Their main hub seems to be in the city we left behind, but it's moving. It's like they're searching for something."

"What are they searching for?" Victoria asked

"My guess, I would say us." Valcheck answered. "I'd say we should probably look to move out in the morning," He turned and regarded Georgia with a dark look on his face. "How is the Professor getting along?"

"He says it shouldn't be too much longer, that it would be ready for the morning," Georgia answered. She had been in to see the Professor and his work before she had come out to speak to Victoria.

"I have a few words to say to him," Valcheck answered. He looked sideways at Max and Victoria. "Are you two right to stay sentry for a bit?"

Max and Victoria nodded, and moved to take their positions back at the walls. Valcheck grabbed Georgia's hand and led her into the manor and through the back door, closing it behind them.

"What did you need to ask the Professor?" Georgia asked as they approached the stairs. Valcheck set his rifle down against the wall in the hall and then turned back to Georgia.

"I lied," he answered, as he bent down and returned Georgia's deep kiss that she given him in the yard. His hands cupped her face as his strong jaw pressed against her feminine frame in a passionate kiss. Georgia returned the kiss deeply, and with her fevered response Valcheck bent down and scooped her up into his arms. Georgia raised herself above him, not breaking their kiss, and wrapped her legs around his strong waist, locking her spreading thighs into place.

Reading the signals loud and clear, Valcheck kept Georgia wrapped around him as he walked purposefully up the stairs. Their feverish kisses never broke as Valcheck's strong and practiced steps ascended them both so easily. At the top of the staircase Valcheck pushed Georgia's back against the wall and she gasped slightly at the impact.

Valcheck let out a sly grin and, knowing Georgia was stable against the wall, moved his right hand up from her bottom and pressed it into her breast. He began to move his fingers as he clutched at her like it was their last moment on Earth. Valcheck began to kiss behind Georgia's ear and then trailed them down her neck and collarbone. Georgia's head rolled backwards and she closed her eyes as she took in the sensation of her lover so close to her.

It wasn't long before his mouth trailed down Georgia's cleavage and his fingers fumbled to undo the buttons on her checked shirt. When he couldn't release the buttons with one hand, Valcheck became impatient and simply pulled at the collar, ripping the buttons free from their holes and springing a few of them to the floor.

Georgia let out an excited gasp and Valcheck's mouth found the top of her bra, his tongue exploring beyond the material, dipping in. A deep rumble escaped his throat in pleasure, and barely containing himself Valcheck moved his lips to meet Georgia's again. As they continued to kiss passionately he lifted Georgia from the wall again and turned, walking down the corridor next to the stairs. He reached the end of the hall where their bedroom was situated and used his right leg to swiftly kick at the wooden door that was closed in front of him.

With a loud thud, the door swang open and splintered slightly, sending a few wood chips flying. With the taste of Georgia on his tongue and a horde of mysterious Visitors making camp not too far from their home, Valcheck didn't even register the broken door. Valcheck strode across his room like he had done a million times before, and with a soft force he deposited his girlfriend on their bed.

Valcheck took in the sight of Georgia sprawled on her back on the bed in front of him, the front of her shirt partially open revealing the soft swell of her breasts beneath her black bra. She was breathing heavily, and he could see the excitement flashing in her brown eyes as she took in Valcheck's hardened and stocky physique.

Georgia's breathing quickened as she moved her fingers to the bottom buttons on her shirt and pulled, ripping the whole thing away from her body. She removed herself from the sleeves and threw it to the side, moving to work on the buttons of her own jeans.

Valcheck grinned down at her and quickly began to shuck his coat and shirt. Georgia moved from pulling her legs out of her jeans and rose to start unbuckling his belt. She kissed the hardened skin and muscle in the shape of a V above the loopholes of his jeans as her slender fingers undid his pants and pulled feverously, springing him free. Georgia put her mouth closer and began to tease him, as Valcheck slowly closed his eyes, and hung his head backwards, enjoying the sensation Georgia was providing him.

As his breathing came faster, he looked down and took in the beautiful woman in front of him, pleasuring him. An almost animalistic groan escaped from his lips and his smirked, hardly believing his luck.

Nothing could stop their pure desire now – not even the end of the world.

****

The group rejoiced that the night was a long one, for it could be the final they would ever see. While Georgia and Valcheck spent it sleeplessly wrapped in each other's arms, it was the looming battle that awaited daybreak that kept the group from rest. Piccolo and the Professor worked relentlessly in the basement on the bombs they were creating out of the Visitors' metallic cuffs, ensuring their readiness to provide the final outcome of the battle. Mia wrestled with her own demons as she tossed and turned in bed, her deceased family once again at the forefront of her mind. She delighted in finding her sister among the ruins of the world, but it stirred up all the feelings that she thought she had long since buried.

Max and Victoria sat together at their guard post, Victoria wrapped in his arms breathing in Max's scent through his duffle coat. Max's fingers slowly encircled hers and traced down her skin to her belly, where their child slept silently, protected inside her. They were relieved of their post at three in the morning, when an unusually dishevelled Nora emerged from the covers of her own bed, trying to shake off the images of Rohan that had been racing through her mind.

The only person who slept soundly that night was Zeke, excited by the prospect of battle after downing a full bottle of whiskey in celebration for the day ahead.

As dawn broke over the desolate world, the group prepared themselves as best they could for the upcoming battle and met in the basement of the house dressed in their survival gear — heavy boots, jeans, and jackets over long-sleeved shirts that covered their body and provided an extra layer of protection when out dealing with the Mindless. They each completed the uniform with their weapons: pistols were stowed in gun belt holders, knives stored down boots, rifles slung over backs, and Visitors' cuffs clamped to their wrists.

Laid out in front of them on the metal bench were the cuffs that each of them had collected from the Visitors and handed over to be turned into weapons to be used against them. Professor Malone and Piccolo had worked tirelessly on expanding the technology of the original cuff and had added wires and extra explosives to the outside of each weapon.

"Is it safe to use with the wires exposed like that?" Victoria asked as she took in the bare bones of the technology, thinking again of her unborn baby. From what she had seen in movies, when it came to explosives the hard-wiring was usually on the inside, encased in metal and protected from the waiting snips of bomb technicians. Professor Malone's explosives were a crazy sheath of wires that looked like exposed muscle running over the metallic casing of the cuff itself.

"When you have a bomb in your hands how safe do you really feel?" Professor Malone pointed out to Victoria. "The metal on the cuff is not like any metal we've ever seen on this planet before so it was almost impossible to hardwire the bomb on the inside because we couldn't even get through to the mechanics of it. What Piccolo and I have done is study and expand the gun that comes out of the cuff and utilised its explosive energy, harnessing it through the wires and setting it to implode in on itself rather than fire outwards. With a bit of added firepower, the spark will ignite and detonate the bomb and everything around it. You place one of these under the Visitors' ships and it will destroy it."

"How long do we have between pressing the button and it exploding?" Valcheck asked the Professor.

"Once ignited it should be almost instantaneous, give or take a few seconds for the firepower from the gun to travel through the wires," the Professor explained. "I've rigged the button so that you can employ it remotely using these buttons", and with that he held up what looked like a battery operated remote control garage door opener. "Press the second button once you're cleared from the ship and you'll light up the sky with firepower."

Upon hearing that, Zeke gave an excited whoop and punched his fist into the sky. "What are we waiting for?" he demanded. "Let's light this candle!"

CHAPTER 9

Standing once again outside in the back garden of the manor, the groups synchronised their watches accordingly and bid their farewells. Nora Dallas watched as the members said emotional goodbyes, knowing that this could be the last time they might see each other.

She watched as Georgia pulled the moody Mia into a hug, who clung to her big sister like a small child. She then pulled away and composed herself, aware of her display of emotional neediness, and reset her rifle over her shoulder. She and Piccolo began to move to the gate and took off in an eastward direction into the trees.

Zeke became restless next to her, shifting from side to side. He was amped for the battle ahead and eager to get started, so Nora saw no other reason to hang around further.

"Let's go!" she told Zeke and nodded to the group before making their way to a second delivery truck that had been parked outside the front of the manor. It had been retrieved from an abandoned road a long time ago with its precious fuel zealously conserved.

As Nora opened the truck's doors to slide in, she looked back at the group. Georgia and Valcheck followed Mia and Piccolo out of the back garden's gate and while Georgia and Valcheck headed north down the sloping hill, Victoria and Max were already hours ahead of them, having left at daybreak to travel to the city. They had the furthest ship to attack.

The plan was for each group to attack the Visitors' ships from different directions, laying the bombs under the ships before exploding them to kingdom come. They all had their own targets laid out in front of them to attack, and each group made their way to their designated ships. Max and Victoria had the furthest to go – heading back into the city they once called their home where the main hub seemed to be.

Across the gulf though, Nora and Zeke had been charged with the opportunity of creating a distraction and drawing as many Visitors to them as possible, clearing the way for the others to plant the bombs under the ships.

Being the distraction was a nerve-racking opportunity, but Nora was ready to swallow her fears and do her part. She was probably going to die today but damned if they wouldn't remember her name in doing so. Nora slid into the truck and started it up, easing it down the sloping hill of the manor.

Behind her she could hear soft grumblings and growling from within the truck's cage and a few thuds as the truck rolled down the driveway and onto the tree-lined street around it. She looked over at Zeke who was sitting in the passenger seat next to her, but he ignored the sounds of the Mindless in the back of their truck as he put a fat cigar to his lips and lit the end with a lighter.

"Hey, give me some of that!" Nora told him and Zeke passed the lit cigar to her. She took a drag and sucked in the smoke, inhaling deeply before blowing out a thinner smoke. "Can't die without one last cigar."

"Who said we're going to die?" Zeke asked in his elongated drawl, reaching for the cigar between Nora's fingers.

"Look around you Z," Nora replied "we're either going to die right here on the battlefield, or be hunted down like dogs if this doesn't work."

"As long as I go down swinging, that'll be good enough for me!" Zeke answered, chipper as ever as he continued to puff on the cigar. Nora shook her head lightly.

She had never seen someone so ready for war.

They drove down the main tree-lined highway for several hours before the next Visitors' ship began to loom in front of them. It was further away from the Visitors' ship that Jay had blown up at the Mt. Beryl Marina and was flanked by two other Visitor ships next to it. It was the largest clump of Visitors in the area and they had seen it as the best place to draw the Visitors into one explosive area with their distractions. Georgia was joining Nora and Zeke from the other side to help plant the bombs under the other two ships and Nora hoped they wouldn't get into too much trouble with the sheer mass of numbers they were facing.

The rest wouldn't be any help, with Max and Victoria heading to the city, and Valcheck, Piccolo and Mia each individually attacking their own ships between the clump and the city. They were all hours apart from each other – help was too far away if they needed it.

Nora breathed in slowly. This certainly felt like the end, but atleast it would go out with a bang rather than a whisper.

Nearing the ship, Nora slowed the truck down and pressed on the break. She could hear their cargo in the back thumping around.

"You ready to run Z?" Nora asked. Zeke looked over to her and picked up his semi-automatic rifle from beside him in the seat.

"I was born ready N!" he laughed. With that Zeke opened the truck door and jumped out, slamming the door behind him. He thumped the side of the door slightly and backed away from the truck, sending the Mindless in the back into groans of attack. Nora eased the truck out of park and continued down the road alone, looking in her rear-view mirror and seeing the camouflage-dressed Zeke taking off into the forest behind her.

Nora continued to drive the truck down the road and soon she began to feel the air around her change. The windows in the truck were down and the air rushing by the fast-moving vehicle stilled, becoming almost stale in the sunny day. The colour of the sun's rays began to change and develop a hazy rust colour in the sky, almost like settling in close to a bushfire.

As Nora rounded a corner she could see the road spread out before her and the Visitors' ship directly in front of her. The air shimmered with its unholy gas and it loomed like the Emerald City. Nora turned the truck and executed a three-point turn so that the truck's rear doors were facing the city. Then she started backing the truck up.

The annoying beeping sound that accompanied trucks backing up blared out into the still air. Nora cursed silently under her breath – Zeke was supposed to have disabled that. She glanced in the rear view mirrors on the side of the truck and could make out a few of the Visitors turning their elongated craniums in her direction.

It was now or never.

Nora quickly stopped the truck and placed it into park, pulling the handbrake. She opened the driver's side door and jumped out, taking her semi-automatic with her. Nora raced around to the back of the truck and pulled the latch that locked the back door. She pushed the door up and was faced with a group of the Mindless, who in unison reached out for her. Nora jumped backwards and grabbed at the latch of the truck, letting down the ramp.

As a group, the decaying Mindless began to stumble towards her, their adrenaline surging and their eyes flashing. Nora jumped backwards out of the way down the road away from the horde which began to stumble down the ramp after her and she pointed her rifle into the air, pulling the trigger and letting off a smattering of bullets into the sky. The sound of the semi-automatic's rapid fire pierced the still air in an almost deafening way, and when the last bullet reverberated into the sky Nora could hear the shrill shrieks of the Visitors behind her.

They were coming for her.

Nora began to make a wide circle around the truck to get out of the way of the Mindless, who were descending the truck's ramp or simply missing the ramp altogether and falling off the side. Several continued to reach for her and surround her as she ducked out of the way and ran to the front, climbing onto the bonnet of the truck and hoisting herself onto the roof.

She took in the surroundings that were being unveiled in front of her and couldn't help but think of Jay, who had done the exact same thing she was doing. Would this be her own kiss of death?

Twenty Visitors were making their way up the road and darting out through the trees on their powerful hind legs. Their eyes flashed a pulsing neon blue ring as they ran straight for the Mindless and for the truck. In front of her the Mindless had emptied out of the truck bed and were spreading out on the road, their adrenaline kicking in at the sight of the Visitors in front of them. The Mindless launched at the living creatures in front of them and the Visitors met them like soldiers on the battlefield, colliding in attack.

Groans and cries ran out through the trees to Nora's left and she saw more of the Mindless stumbling out from the tree line towards the Visitors, supernaturally sensing in their beating hearts and wanting to devour them. The Mindless had thick rusted chains attached around their necks which clambered as they ran towards the Visitors and attacked.

Nora watched as at the edge of the tree line, close to the Visitor's ship, where Zeke darted out of the woods in his camouflage gear. As part of their plan for maximum attack the group had tied up Mindless and hidden them among the trees with the chains around their necks and Zeke had freed them to help with the distraction against the Visitors. All along the roads, the other survivors were doing the same.

Nora watched as Zeke closed in on his target and shimmered like a mirage as he forced his way closer to the ship.

By now the Mindless and the Visitors were locked in a heated battle before her, and Nora pressed the buttons that Victoria had shown her on her metallic cuff to release the Visitors' gun. The cuff transformed into its gun and Nora looked out across the battlefield. The Visitors were greatly outnumbered, even with the five Mindless banging against the front of the truck and trying to reach for Nora instead, having been aware of her own hammering pulse. Mindless were hanging off the thick ropey limbs of the Visitors in groups of two and three and the Visitors struggled to push them off as they sunk their bloodied mouths into flailing arms and shoulders.

A few Visitors had successfully disposed of several of the Mindless, who lay clumped in a mass of body parts and guts all over the road. Nora watched as a Visitor let out a blood curdling roar as a Mindless bit into its hind legs from where it lay, itself legless on the ground. The Visitor swiped at the legless Mindless with raw power and backhanded it straight into one of the trees. Blood splattered and its spine crunched as the Mindless fell wetly to the ground. Seemingly undaunted, the Mindless crawled back towards the Visitor, dragging its bloody mess of damaged spine and tattered entrails behind it, as the Visitor began to convulse, shaking and falling to the ground before it.

They were turning.

Nora took aim as the Visitor suddenly stopped convulsing. It sprang up into the air with a mighty blow and Nora fired the gun straight into the Mindless Visitor's head, imploding its mind in green ooze. The rest of the torso fell limply to the floor where it has just been lying.

Perturbed by the sudden demise of its prey, the dragging Mindless found its way to another Visitor lying on the ground. Its body was motionless, but the clear mucus- like substance that usually reattached its limbs was being secreted instead from its abdomen, healing a deep wound there. The Mindless reached the Visitor's arm and chomped down, causing an almighty shriek to fill the air; the Visitor began to shake and shudder in response.

Nora aimed at the Mindless and fired, splattering the rest of its blood and matter onto the concrete of the road, freeing it from a life of dragging its worthless spine around. She then aimed her gun to the Mindless Visitor who was convulsing noisily next to it and fired, decimating it instantly.

Again and again, the Mindless attacked the Visitors and the undead numbers were lost in the melee, too many to count. Nora fired the Visitors' own weapon on them time after time, before she briefly looked back at where Zeke had last shimmered off to, into the distance to the Visitors' ship. The whole area was now crawling with another twenty or so Visitors as they came to join the battle from the other ships.

More groans were stifled from behind the Visitors' shrills and shrieks and Nora saw more Mindless emerging from behind the ship and from the trees. This was the second wave that Georgia was bringing in.

That was when she saw him.

Emerging from the woods was Rohan. Nora could recognise him anywhere due to the fact that he was always in the back of her mind, his face haunting her daily as she wondered what had happened to him. Now she knew.

Rohan was still wearing the duffle coat and dark pants that he had been wearing the day that he had locked her in the trunk of that car. His dark skin was surprisingly clean but his clothes were splattered with blood. He had a fresh looking bite wound on the side of his face and was missing an ear. In a sheath attached to his belt was the same blood-rusted tyre iron he had used to fight his way away from the car boot he had locked her in.

Based on how fresh he seemed, Nora felt her heart sink into her stomach. Now she knew the truth – he had truly abandoned her in the trunk of that car and had never bothered to return for her.

But while Nora felt disappointment at the betrayal of her friend, she was surprised to find herself feeling sorry for him. He thought he could get away and here he was, one of the Mindless. He thought that Nora would slow him down, but it was he who was the weak one – the one that was decaying while Nora stood strong.

If only he had listened; if only he cared. Nora's heart went out to him, but the grief was not complete. She didn't mourn this Rohan, she pitied him.

The Mindless Rohan was walking slowly out of the woods and Nora noticed a big rusty metal collar angled around his thick neck. He dragged a thick chain behind him on the ground and she realised that Rohan was one of the Mindless that Georgia had found and strung up in the woods by the collars and chains, ready to release them as a distraction.

Georgia had found him. Nora couldn't help but think that if she had told her about Rohan, told her she was still looking for him, at least she could have ended her constant fears for him. Perhaps they could have found him the same way they searched for Mia. If Nora had been honest from the start, maybe he would have even been alive and unharmed, and they could have saved him. In that moment Nora resolved to be more honest and open to her comrades in arms – if they survived the battle that is.

But it also dawned on Nora that there was never any possibility of saving Rohan – even when he had been alive and well and employed as her bodyguard. He was always destined for nothing more than decay. It was simply in his disregarding, selfish nature.

The ambling Rohan reached out with an opened and gasping mouth, taking in the battle and shaping his adrenaline. Nora looked at the ship before her and saw a Visitor climb down the side of the ship on its suction cupped fingers and pass through the shimmering gas emanating from the ship's side.

Where were Zeke and Georgia?

The Visitor climbing down the side of the ship seemed different. It was larger, and more reserved than the others that had raced into the battle that was unfolding in a seemingly slow motion in front of her.

Then she saw its cuff.

The metallic cuff that the Visitor was wearing was glowing in a neon stripe of green. Nora looked down at her own cuff clasped to her wrist and saw the deep underside glow of neon blue, strikingly different to this Visitor's green one. Nora knew instantly that this Visitor was one that was special. It was the one in charge.

The Commander.

The Commander was elegant, fast and agile, moving with more specific pace and speed that suggested a higher intelligence. As Nora watched the Commander close the distance in the battlefield she registered that the now surging Rohan was actually the closest Mindless to the Commander. Despite her resolve, her heart leapt into her throat as Rohan gnashed his teeth in the Commander's direction, racing towards him for a bite.

As Rohan reached the Commander, Nora watched in horror as the Visitor in charge leisurely put its three suction cupped fingers against Rohan's skull where his ear had been and pulled, dragging the skin forward. From where she stood on the roof of the truck, she could make out the fresh blood and gore of Rohan's face as the Commander, in a motion that a skilled rabbit skinner would have applauded, pulled Rohan's skin off in one strong dragging motion, removing his mouth, lips, cheeks and nose, revealing muscle and bone and gleaming chattering teeth underneath.

Rohan continued to gnash his bare teeth at the Commander, despite the dark skin on his face being ripped off and flung to the ground in a pile of gore. All that was left of his face were his gnashing teeth, his popping eyes, his forehead and nose, which had partially been removed leaving a gaping hole. His once charming dark chocolate eyes flashed with the red rim of the Mindless as he snarled and the Commander held him back easily with one suction-cupped hand.

Nora watched in horror as this powerful Visitor raised the gun that had descended from its metallic cuff and placed it squarely under what was left of Rohan's bloody chin. The Commander fired and the brilliant blue electricity darted straight into Rohan's skull from below, decimating him in one dramatic shot that was almost so fast that Nora couldn't quite catch the flash. What was left of Rohan's duffle-clad torso after his head exploded from his body sank to its knees and then to the street in a heap.

Nora couldn't breathe. This had once been her best friend, and while he had been a snake for leaving her in that boot, it had led her to Valcheck and the others. It had led to her survival. Despite all of her anger at being abandoned, without him, she wouldn't have made it this far and learnt so much about herself.

In response, Nora felt the world around her pulse black like she was about to pass out.

She had regularly dreamt of her revenge, wrestling between the notion of protecting Rohan and hurting him, but she had never wanted revenge to be like that.

A thud pulled Nora out of her stupor and she looked around. The truck was being rocked by the Mindless and she saw a Mindless Visitor climbing to the roof from the back of the truck's hood in front of her. Yet again, she had let her guard down and become distracted because of Rohan.

Nora focused on the task at hand and fired her readied semi-automatic at the Mindless Visitor, the force of the shot sending the creature backwards off the end of the truck. Nora calmly walked towards the back and in a blind haze began shooting downwards, killing the Mindless that had followed her and not joined in the battle. Around her Mindless and Visitors were still fighting and she trained her gun on them one after the other.

Another thud landed behind her and Nora turned quickly from her position. She raised her gun instinctively and was about to fire before she took in that it was Georgia climbing up onto the roof.

"It's just me!" Georgia cried, "They're all loose and attacking the Visitors and I placed the two other bombs on the other ships. Has Zeke come back yet? Have you seen him?"

"I don't know, should he be done by now" Nora answered, as she turned back towards the battle raging in front of them. Georgia steadied herself next to Nora and turned on her own gun strapped to her wrist.

"Did you see the one with the green cuff?" Georgia asked as she helped Nora fire off against the Mindless Visitors that were changing in front of them. Blood and brain matter covered the street like it was raining gore.

"Yeah, I saw it rip through Rohan like he was tissue paper," Nora answered. Georgia stopped for a moment.

"Who is Rohan?" She asked. Only Valcheck had been told the whole story.

"He's … just someone I used to know," Nora replied, "He betrayed me."

"Good riddance to him then!" Georgia cried as she continued to fire, too distracted by the war waging below them to take in her friend's hesitant stupor. "Look, there's Zeke!" Georgia cried, pointing out towards the street where Zeke was running, shimmering slightly as he passed through the mirage of gas in front of the ship. Nora turned in that direction and gasped in horror, realising that the Commander stood in between Zeke and the safety of the tree line.

As Zeke ran down the street towards the trees he fired a round of bullets into the left shoulder of the Commander that was blocking his way, still perched over Rohan's fallen body. The Commander let out a roar and looked backwards as Nora could see the silvery mucus beginning to cover the bullet hole in its shoulder already. The Commander raised its right arm towards Zeke and its cuff on its wrist pulsed a disturbing neon green.

With the raising of its suction cupped hand, Zeke began to levitate off his feet and into the air, still floating in the direction he had been running in. His body became frozen and rigid as it was lifted in the air and his face muscles twitched as he tried to fight against the pull of being lifted off the ground.

Zeke began to convulse violently and his dark skin began to spread into an even darker colour as blood leaked through his pores, staining his clothes red and covering his entire body like he had been dunked into a bucket of blood. It dripped off his feet in thick pools from where he levitated in the air and shook droplets of blood off of him as he convulsed.

Suddenly, in a brilliant bloody-motion, Zeke's body exploded, splattering everything nearby. Pools of dark red blood formed on the concrete below him and covered the trees nearby. Hunks of Zeke's skin and formless flesh fell to the ground and covered the road.

Miraculously the Commander didn't get a single blood droplet or piece of flesh on itself as it dropped its reaching suction cupped fingers, satisfied with its work.

From where she stood on the top of the truck, Nora screamed like a banshee. She had just watched two of her best friends die within moments of each other in a horrifying way – both at the hands of this leader. It was all finally too much for her.

The Commander turned away from the bloody mess that was Zeke and looked in the direction of Nora's scream – its flashing blue eyes locking on to Nora's wide horrified ones.

"I didn't know they can do that!" Nora cried in disbelief, gasping.

Georgia grabbed Nora's arm. "We need to blow the ships now. Do you have the detonators?" she practically screamed in panic to Nora. Nora was stunned.

"Uh ... I ... yeah..." she stammered. "Is it time yet?" she asked

Georgia looked at the Commander that had started making its way up the road towards them. It passed the debris and decay and chaos without as much as a glance, like it had seen the horrors of war all before. In front of them, the last of the Visitors were turning but the Commander only had eyes for them.

"It doesn't matter. They need to blow now!" Georgia cried, as she pulled Nora towards the front of the truck and jumping onto the bonnet. She slid off the smooth metal and onto the hard ground next to her before she opened the driver's side door. Nora followed suit, kicking a stray Mindless out of the way with her chunky black combat boots before landing on the tarmac. She ripped open the passenger side door and jumped in as Georgia revved the engine and they lurched forward. The opened doors and lowered ramp from the trucks bed rattled and shook before the ramp burst off its hinges in a glow of sparks, bounced and landed on the road behind them.

Nora looked out of the passenger side window at the chaos they were leaving behind and saw the Commander continuing to follow them like a terminator but then stop suddenly. It turned its long cranium to one side and then in a flash took off towards the trees, disappearing completely from sight.

"Blow it Nora!" Georgia cried as the truck rounded the corner fast, almost spilling onto its side. Nora reached into the back pocket of her jeans and pulled out three of the garage door remotes. She pressed the buttons as fast as possible and waited for the almost instantaneous explosions that would blast the Visitors back into space.

CHAPTER 10

As the day had broken and the sun had risen, Victoria and Max walked out of the woods and onto an overgrown back road. It was a different road to the one that they had been walking down when they were first brought to the manor, but they had retrieved a car they saw had been abandoned on the side of the road, filled it with gasoline that Professor Malone had spare in his laboratory, and had deposited it at the edge of the woods for use in the attack. The car they had left for themselves was a dark green Jeep with black canvas roofing; the pine scented air freshener dangling from the mirror looking incongruous in this situation.

Max slid behind the wheel and put the key he had pocketed into the ignition while Victoria slid into the passenger seat and put her satchel bag at her feet. Max turned the engine over and pulled out onto the road heading in the direction away from the Visitors. They drove in silence for a long time, hours passing as the wind whipped at the canvas roof of the jeep, and the group rose from their beds for their own day of battle.

"I still don't think you should have come Victoria," Max told her quietly. "You should have stayed back at the manor with the Professor."

"And leave all the fun to everyone else? Not a chance!" Victoria replied dryly. She and Max had had this conversation the night before while they had been acting as sentries for the manor.

"You're not like everyone else though ... Not in this situation," Max told her, his worry getting the better of him.

"Because I'm pregnant?" Victoria turned to face her husband in her seat. "Max, we talked about this. The Visitors' are trying to take over the world – our world – if we don't do something, if we don't stop them, then we are all as good as dead anyway. It won't be a world worth bringing a child into. We need all the help we can get to win this war."

Max sighed deeply. His wife was so headstrong, and while she would do anything for her family she would also do anything to help others as well – to help the earth. . There was no changing her mind last night while they prepared for battle at their sentinel posts, and there was no changing her mind now.

"Well I don't want you to be the one to lay the bomb alright?" Max told her, "I don't want you anywhere near it."

This time Victoria sighed and turned towards the window next to her. "Don't worry, I've got you covered," she told him. She would be in the fight no matter what, but if Max really wanted to be the one to get close to the Visitors' ship she would allow that. The idea of getting close and personal to the ship flooded her mind with images of brilliant blue light, of her chainsaw whirring through the tree-trunk-like neck of the Visitor, its green brain matter splattering on her, the red glow that stared out from the dark and vacant eyes of the Mindless Visitor.

Suddenly Victoria was filled with the same pain that she had felt that day at the marina. She closed her eyes and saw nothing but white hot light behind her eyelids, and the pain coming from her womb seemed to course through her veins. She gasped and clutched at stomach, her bright mind filling with images of the Visitors she had encountered.

Somehow, Victoria remembered how the pain had subsided at the marina and she struggled to remain in control, waiting for relief. She focused on her breathing as it was the only thing she was able to do, and slowly the dazzling blue lights subsided into the dark black holes of the Mindless Visitor's eyes, rimmed with red where the iris should be. Her vision became dark before she realised she was looking at the back of her eyelids. The pain inside her began to subside and she was left with a wave of nausea that felt like morning sickness again.

Victoria opened her eyes and blinked against the natural light, suddenly too bright to comprehend.

"Are you ok?" Max asked, worried, glancing over at her from the driver's seat.

Victoria let out the breath she hadn't been aware she had been holding. "Yes, I am fine. It's just morning sickness."

"I thought you were starting to get over that," Max replied tersely, still obviously worried.

"I don't know. It comes and goes. I'll be fine," Victoria answered. She turned away from her husband and leaned her hot, sweaty head against the cool of the car windowpane. She watched the trees zoom by as Max drove the car down the highway, the nausea beginning to subside.

What did all of this mean? Without the proper equipment and access to trained doctors and midwives, Victoria's pregnancy was in no way normal. She hadn't had an ultrasound, or found out if her child had all its fingers and toes in the way it was supposed to. It was only from the muffled movements inside her and the swelling of her belly did she even know the child was alive and so essentially healthy.

So this 'morning sickness' was a scary process. It was nothing like what she had read about and heard about back when the world functioned normally, and Victoria worried that Georgia had been right when she suggested that the Visitor that had compelled her when she tried to save Ian had perhaps left something more long-lasting to impact the foetus.

Max took a turn in the road that saw them travelling in a northern direction. As another hour passed on the road Victoria saw no reason to worry about the morning sickness now. Everything could be over in a minute anyway – she'd take it up with her husband after the battle.

If they survived it.

It wasn't long before Max and Victoria started the drive into the city that once been their home. Nothing much had changed from how they had left it in the wake of the first attack, with buildings left crumbling and abandoned to nature and her greedy qualities. Cars were left as hunks of rusting metal on the sides of the roads and belongings were scattered, withering away into nothing. Victoria was hit with a strong nostalgia as she watched the life they had left behind roll past her window.

It wasn't long before they neared the apartment building that they have lived in, where the first settlement had begun and had changed their world again. Victoria had to shake her head to clear it of the images of her compulsion, scared that her 'morning sickness' would hit her like a wave again.

She couldn't battle that inside her. Not now. Not while they had another battle to take up swords for.

Max angled the Jeep towards the apartment building that used to be their home and Victoria saw the Visitor's ship begin to rise into her vision. The Visitors' ship was just like all the others they had seen – round, metallic, and leaking otherworldly gas into the air. But this ship seemed haunted, nestled in its own crater surrounded by the bare bones of the first settlement's craft. They had destroyed it in an almighty explosion, and Victoria knew that the Visitors in this ship were not happy with the remains that had been left behind.

Max began to slow the car down with only a few roads between them and the apartment building where the new ship sat. He did a quick U-turn so that the car was now facing the way they had just came. He turned the ignition off and they both slid out of the Jeep. Victoria gave Max the strap of the satchel bag that held the bombs and he pulled it over his neck, crossing the strap across his torso. He in turn handed Victoria his rifle that he had placed in the back seat of the Jeep, and she slid the strap of the gun over her right shoulder.

With their gear in place they began the walk up the road they had wandered along so many times, cracks now forming in the concrete beneath their feet. They made their way towards an office building up a hill that was still standing, not far up the road to the left from their old home and from the Visitors' ship. Careful where they walked, they both had their pistols drawn and at the ready should they come across any of the Mindless wandering their way through the desolate roads.

They heard them before they saw them.

Chained to the handrail of a staircase next to a building were three of the Mindless, growling and grumbling under their breath. They each wore thick, rusted metal collars around their necks that were chained together to the metal railing.

Victoria took in the creatures as they approached. There was a short platinum blonde girl with large brown eyes that stared hungrily at her with red rimmed irises. She had been gorgeous in life, but the decay of her body had made her round face hollow and sunken. She was caked in dirt and blood and the rusted collar dug into her neck as she strained to reach Victoria, breaking the skin. Next to her was a girl with long dark hair and large lips that were cracked with dried congealed blood. Her right eyeball was missing and the hole around her eye was dark, exposing muscle and tendons. She looked like she had fallen victim to some birds during the attack, making Victoria wonder about the pests that would have taken her eye from her. Next to the two girls was a man with a Middle Eastern appearance in a buttoned down shirt and jeans, his jet black pompadour reminiscent of old times. His almost grey eyes flashed with the red rimmed iris of the Mindless as he outstretched a bloodied and rotten hand that had fingers missing from it.

Max circled the stairs and unchained the Mindless, whose adrenaline surged as they reached out for Victoria standing in front of them. The collars around their neck bit into their rotting flesh and held them back as they tried with all of their might to reach their pray. Max pulled the chain backwards and they stumbled with it, falling in behind him at a safe distance, though still grumbling and gnashing for a taste of their flesh.

"Let's go!" Max said to Victoria and they continued their walk around the office building, wary of their new comrades as they grumbled behind them, trying to pull against the collars and damaging their necks further through their decayed skin.

After a short while Victoria could feel the air pressure begin to change, like a storm was coming. There was an almost electrical feeling in the air and everything felt stale despite being outside. There was no breeze, but the sky above the city was a rusty dust colour, almost creating a halo around the Visitors' ships.

They were getting close.

Several once-specimen trees in the front of the office building had fallen down, splintered at the trunk as though hit by lightning. The fronts of the trees were charred black, like they were burnt on one side and the leaves had blown away from the area, leaving nothing but dark dirt. Max and Victoria stepped gingerly onto the dirt and walked into this part of the barren wasteland of once-manicured lawn.

Max and Victoria reached the edge of the dirt area and moved onto the overgrown lawn of the office building, situated at the front of the small hill with a tremendous lookout over the once bustling road beneath. They neared a burnt and twisted hedge that encircled the unkempt lawn in this area and Max tied the chains of the Mindless to a nearby splintered tree, securing them in place.

He and Victoria bent low behind the hedge and peaked over the edge. Max unhooked the strap of the bag from around him and took the rifle from Victoria and brought the sights up to his eye, levelling the gun in front of him.

In front of them, the Visitors' ship loomed large. It was just as Victoria had remembered – a large oval-shaped metallic ship with the same glowing blue lights and unearthly gas shimmering in the air underneath it. The ground beneath the ship had been thoroughly decimated and there was not a living plant anywhere near the circle of the ship's underbelly. Victoria could see the Visitors working on the ship, crawling around it on their muscular grey legs. There was roughly fifteen of them busying themselves around the ship, their large oval-shaped craniums moving this way and that, their beak-like mouths opening and shutting with short piercing sounds.

"There's not many of them outside. Do you think they are inside or on scouting missions?" Max asked as he peaked through the sight of the rifle and took in the ship.

"Let's hope they are inside," Victoria answered as she checked her watch. "Five minutes," she told Max.

"Be careful ok?" Max told her as he lowered the gun and set it softly in the long grass they were kneeling in. He turned to his wife and pulled her face into his with both hands, kissing her passionately. Victoria returned the kiss hungrily.

It could very well be their last.

Max pulled away but paused, her head still in his hands. His blue eyes danced between her brown eyes as he took her in.

"I'm going to get closer so when it starts there won't be much ground to cover. Good luck!" He dropped his hands from her face and grabbed the satchel bag at his feet, slinging it back over his shoulder. Max walked over to the three Mindless at the tree and unchained them once again, leading them off along the burnt and overgrown edge of the hedge line, keeping low to the ground and stepping as quickly and as quietly as possible given his grumbling entourage. Victoria watched him round the hedges and the office building before she turned to the task at hand and pressed the buttons on the metallic cuff she had put back on her left wrist. The hidden weapon inside descended into place, and she readied herself, resting the barrel of the Visitors' gun against the spikey remnants of the hedge.

An adrenaline seemed to hum inside her as she steeled herself. Victoria aimed at one of the Visitors near the edge of the clearing on the other side of the ship, and waited.

Suddenly, the Visitors turned their heads to the left in unison and opened their beak-like mouths, making a shrill shriek that pierced Victoria's brain. It surprised Victoria to realise that these Visitors must all be somehow connected, as they were probably now aware of the attack that Nora was leading far away near the manor. A high pitched wailing noise emanated from the ship and the Visitors crouched on their thick ropey legs, poised to fight.

Their legs kicked into gear and several of the Visitors that had been outside the ship took off towards the attack Nora and Zeke were leading hours away. Many stayed behind poised and at the ready for an attack, but Victoria found herself wondering how much ground they could cover in a short time period. Would they reach the other ships quickly, despite the fact that they were days of walking away?

It was now or never.

With the distraction in place, Max pushed the three Mindless creatures out from his hiding place at the side of the road where he had headed after their kiss. The Mindless still wore the collars and dragged their rusted chains behind them, but they had now been freed. They stumbled up the road and saw the Visitor closest to Max poised at the ready. The adrenaline of the Mindless kicked in and the platinum blonde started running towards the Visitor.

The sounds from the road below were almost deafening as the Mindless growled and the Visitor let out a high-pitched scream. The blonde Mindless sunk its bloodied mouth deep into the mottled grey flesh of the Visitor, barely making a dent as the Visitor pushed it off in one swoop of its large arm. The blonde went flying, landing on its back on the ground just as the Middle Eastern man with the pompadour reached the Visitor and began tearing into its arm.

The shrieks continued, and the other Visitors that had stayed at the ship took off towards the group being attacked, ready to help defend against their own creations. The eyeless dark-haired Mindless, energised by rampant adrenaline, reached the next Visitor easily and began the attack, while the blonde shuffled back to her feet, reaching out for living flesh.

Shrieks and shrills filled the air, and Victoria watched as the congealed purple blood of the Mindless mixed with the green ooze of the Visitors. The first Visitor who had been attacked by the man with the pompadour had fallen, while the Mindless man tore wildly at its abdomen. It began to convulse violently, flinging the Middle Eastern man off sideways easily in a spectacular flying motion towards a towering tree that had managed to escape unscathed in the constant battle that took place around it.

With the Visitors being attacked by the Mindless, Max started out from behind a building, running as fast as he could towards the ship. He steered clear of the battle as he got closer to the ship, pulling a bandana tied around his neck up to his mouth as he avoided the shimmering pockets of the unearthly gas streaming down the side of the ship. Max slid the last metre on his side and slipped into the crater beneath the ship, righting himself and pulling the bomb out from inside his bag.

Meanwhile the first Visitor had been turned. Its convulsions had ceased and it was thrashing around to get to its feet. Even from where she hid, Victoria could easily see the red rims pulsing from inside the dark holes that were the eyes of the Visitor.

Victoria sprang into action and levelled the Visitors' gun directly at its head. It let out a deafening roar as she fired, the kick of the gun no longer affecting her but still making her hair stand on end. Despite the distance away on the hill, the Mindless Visitors' head imploded from the electrical bullets, and green brain-like matter splattered against the concrete of the street behind it. The Mindless Visitor slumped backwards and lay motionless on the ground.

Around the Mindless Visitor, the others were turning too. The brunette Mindless was still clinging to a Visitor's muscular back as it tried to fling her off, and another had started convulsing near the blonde, who had gotten to her feet, struggling as she was now missing her right arm.

Methodically, Victoria turned to each Mindless Visitor and fired their own weapon on them, splattering the battlefield with entrails, purple-grey blood and green brain matter.

With all of the Visitors turned into Mindless there was no chance that the other-worldly creatures would regenerate themselves again. Victoria turned her gun towards the Mindless blonde with one arm and the eyeless brunette and fired before she lifted her eyes from the battlefield and searched around for Max.

He was running away from the ship towards her, his mouth still covered with the bandana and the satchel bag slapping against his backside as he ran. Victoria smiled at the success of the mission, and pressed the buttons on the cuff, lodging the gun away inside. Her hair still felt like it was still standing on end as she reached into her pocket and thumbed the garage door opener that would ignite the bombs that Max had readied under the Visitors' ship.

Suddenly, Victoria heard a crunch behind her and turned with a gasp. She looked straight into the dark black eyes of a Visitor. It was the Captain of these Visitors from another planet and it towered before her on its hind legs, its skin mottled and its muscles moving as it let out a low growl from its beak-like throat.

Victoria's eyes widened in terror and took in what the Captain was holding in its suction cupped fingers.

It was her chainsaw.

It was covered in the congealed purple blood of the Visitor that Victoria had rammed the chainsaw's blade into. It was rusted and old, but there was no mistaking her favourite weapon that she had left behind.

Victoria's eyes bounced from her chainsaw and back to the Captain, whose own eyes glowed with a brilliant bright blue. Victoria felt the energy and the adrenaline from the light seep into her pores, and she felt instantly drained of feeling, frozen. She felt the trance of the Captain take hold of her and somewhere inside her womb the pain she had been feeling seemed to flow through her veins like it had replaced her blood.

Victoria didn't know what was the worse – the feeling of compulsion from the Captain, or the feeling of pain from her unborn child. The world around her swam in white hot light and soon the feeling of both was all she knew.

CHAPTER 11

The explosions rocked the very earth that Max stood on, but nothing shook him to the core like finding his wife missing.

He had run away from the Visitors' ship at speed, breathing hard through the confining material of the bandana tied around his mouth to protect him from the gases emanating from the ship. The empty satchel bag slammed against his lower back as he ran after having planted the bomb that Professor Malone had designed under the ship. He puffed hard as he ran up the hill and towards the lawn of the office building where he had left Victoria.

But she was gone.

Max stopped and looked around, calling her name, but there was no sign of her. He pulled the bandana down from around his mouth and called her name again. He looked down to where she had been sitting to find her loaded pistol lying in the long grass next to the hedge she had hid behind.

Around the hedge the grass had been disturbed and he saw large footprints in the bent grass blades that headed back off towards the side of the office building Max had left just moments prior. It was a sure sign that something untoward had happened.

Max took in the full gravity of the situation just as his watched started beeping, set on a timer for when the first explosions near the manor were to go off. They were far away – almost invisible here in the city where Max stood – but if everything had gone well with the others than the Visitors' ships would be nothing but smouldering metal and fiery debris.

Max looked out at the Visitors' ship standing in front of him. It was still intact because Victoria was the one who had the remote control that would detonate the bombs. The plan had been for them to rendezvous back at the office building and press the button to ignite the bomb as they made their escape. They would then rush back to the manor where they would put out any spot fires that may threaten their home and pick off any leftover Mindless or Mindless Visitors.

Taking in the unexploded bomb, Max knew instantly that he had failed the mission, and failed the group's plan.

But more importantly, he had failed to protect his wife and their unborn child.

It was then that he saw her. A Visitor was leading the way back to the ship he had just placed the bomb under. Its large muscled hind legs moved quickly as it made its way back to the ship with what looked like a rusted chainsaw in its suction cupped fingers. Victoria was trailing behind it in a stupor – her eyes glowing blank and blue, her body under the will of the Captain. Max had seen this before, back when Victoria had attempted to save Ian Peters from the Visitor in their old apartment building, and the Visitor had taken Victoria instead.

She had survived once, she could survive again.

But Max held his breath as he watched the Captain move towards the opening of the ship, leading Victoria inside. Max knew that if Victoria was to go inside, he may never find her again. Who knew what was inside the ship? Besides, he needed her to press the remote control to ignite the bombs he had placed. She couldn't do that from inside the ship – she would die.

Thinking quickly, Max reached down and grabbed the rifle that Victoria had left at the base of the hedge. He rose the sights to his eyes and levelled the barrel of the gun towards the Captain leading his wife into the ship below. He aimed, took in a deep breath and squeezed the trigger.

The bullet went straight through the shoulder of the Captain and the power behind it forced it to sway in place. It righted itself and turned in Max's direction letting out a wailing screech of a sound. Behind it, Victoria stopped dead in her tracks and swayed as well, a look of pain on her face. It was then he realised that while Victoria was under the Captain's spell, she would feel whatever he would do to it.

He was causing pain to Victoria as well.

From where he stood Max saw the bullet wound in the Captain's shoulder begin to shimmer with a mucus-like membrane as it covered the hole and began to heal itself. The Captain's dark cavernous eyes continued to search the hill for him but Max hid behind the hedge once more, feeling strangled at the idea of being able to do nothing to help Victoria, not while she was connected to the Captain.

Max peaked back over the hedge and that the bullet wound was almost completely healed and the Captain turned angrily away with a grunt and pulled one of its suction cup fingers around Victoria's shoulders, who was standing behind it. It pulled her roughly in front of it so that Victoria blocked the Captain from Max's waiting bullets. Then both Victoria and the Captain continued walking towards the ship, up the ramp and disappeared into its dark metallic recesses.

Max's mind raced. He felt helpless as he watched a Visitor from another world lead his wife away into an otherworldly ship. He thought of getting up and rushing down to the ship, firing his way through and taking his wife back, but as regular

Visitors they would always heal and with Victoria still compelled they would both be goners. He could go back and get the others, but they were hours away and they had their own work to do in the battlefield. In that time, the Captain could take the ship and leave the Earth with Victoria still inside.

No, he had failed this mission and he failed his wife. He needed to act now.

Max watched in horror as another Visitor emerged down the road from the other side of the ship. It marched with a purpose and he noticed that its dark eyes were rimmed in blue. Something about this Visitor seemed powerful – almost leader-like – and as he took in a pulsing neon green that glowed from the cuff on its wrist, Max knew the different colour confirmed his suspicions. This leader unceremoniously entered the Visitors' ship by the same ramp that the Captain had taken Victoria up, and Max knew this was a bad sign.

It was then that the idea popped into Max's mind. He could use the same plan the group had used to distract and turn the Visitors so that they were easier to kill. It had worked several times before and it meant he could work the plan right now. It was the only thing he could do.

Max scanned the area for the Mindless that he had drawn into the battlefield to begin with. He could see the blonde Mindless lying in a heap with a missing arm and a bloody stump, and near her was the eyeless brunette lying spreadeagled on the concrete. Victoria must have taken them out. Max's eyes darted around looking for the Middle Eastern man and found him impaled by a large tree branch that stuck out all the way through his chest and kept him pinned to the trunk of the tree. He was slumped forward, bloodied around his mouth and the hole in his chest, but he was moaning softly with the adrenaline leaving his body.

He would do, but Max knew that numbers were what would help him get Victoria back.

Max jumped up from his position behind the hedge and listened. He closed his eyes and strained his ears into the world around him. He could hear the soft crackling of fire and the soft humming of the gas seeping from the Visitors' ship in front of him. He strained his ears further and finally heard it – a moan that carried through the stale air.

The Mindless in the area that hadn't been recruited into the battle had been alerted to the activity and were on their way to them.

Max opened his eyes and sprang into action, running through the grass over the soft earth in the direction he had heard the Mindless in. He ran behind the office building and ran up the street behind the action, his eyes scouring the abandoned buildings for movement before he found them.

They were wandering down the street together, ambling. At the sound of his approaching feet slapping on the concrete the Mindless turned in his direction and started to groan louder.

Max baulked for a minute. There were two of them, but their size and appearance caught him off guard. They were both well-built men and Max was struck because both of them looked like hardened survivors.

One was tall with blonde spikey hair that was longer on top and he had a five o'clock shadow. He was dressed in dirt-caked shorts and a t-shirt, and had a single bloodied bite mark on his forearm that had congealed somewhat. It was a relatively clean bite and it gave Max the impression that he had been able to fight the offending Mindless off quite easily. The other man was slightly shorter with a defined muscular build. He wore a long-sleeved black shirt and shorts and had black hair that was longer on top and shorter at the sides. This Mindless hadn't gotten away as cleanly as the taller one had as Max could see a huge chunk of flesh torn from his calf muscle. The split muscle and meat in his leg was ragged and bloody, but wasn't bleeding, suggesting that they hadn't just been bitten.

Despite the congealed blood and flesh on these Mindless, they still had an appearance of recent cleanliness. They seemed like they had found somewhere safe relatively nearby to hole up prior to being attacked. Max judged quickly that they might be a part of a community and that whatever happened to them must have been a recent attack – later than when Nora and Zeke had gone out reaping Mindless for the distractions, but earlier than the battle.

This meant that there could be others currently battling the Visitors and the Mindless.

But Max couldn't think about the others right now. He had a wife and baby to save and a Visitors' ship to blow up, whether others were involved or not.

Thinking quickly as the Mindless before him began to groan louder and louder, their eyes flashing with their red-rimmed irises, Max started backing away down the road towards the office building he had just run from.

"Come get me!" he screamed at the Mindless before he turned on his heel and started to run back the way he came. The Mindless groans behind him turned into a roar and the adrenaline from the virus kicked in. He could hear the two Mindless men running towards him at full speed, their feet stomping on the cracked concrete.

As Max rounded the office building again he had a brief look behind him and saw that while the black-haired Mindless was behind due to the damage in its calf, the spikey-haired blonde was almost upon him. Max concentrated in doubling his speed as he reached the area that Victoria had been taken from and used his momentum to propel himself across the grass and over the hedge they had hidden behind. With the Mindless still following him, Max took off down the hill towards the ship.

There weren't any more Visitors around the ship and the air was as still as a tomb, but Max could barely take any of it in as he raced at top speed down the hill towards the metal hulk. He broke off to the side to approach the Middle Eastern man pinned to the tree, who reached out towards him with a muffled groan as Max closed in, slowing his pace as he reached the tree. With its arms outstretched reaching for him and its teeth gnashing, Max grabbed the Mindless by the shoulders and pulled with all his might. The Mindless was dragged forward and the tree branch started slipping back through the hole in its chest with a slick sliding sound. Blood started spurting from the hole as the Mindless man stumbled forward, no longer rooted into the tree but still trying to reach for Max.

Max quickly dropped his hold on the Mindless man's shoulders and looked behind him, seeing the spikey-haired blonde and the shorter black-haired Mindless torpedoing down the hill, tripping and stumbling slightly with the sudden decline of the earth below them. Max took off towards the entrance of the ship in front of him, aware now of the groans and stumbles of the Middle Eastern Mindless man he had just freed from the tree as it too followed him.

Max ran up the ramp, his boots clomping and making a hollow yet steely sound on the metal. He clicked the buttons on the Visitors' cuff that he wore on his right wrist and freed the gun inside the cuff without missing a beat.

Max entered the metallic ship and rose into instant darkness. The air around him changed from being stale to a metallic cold – almost like walking into a metal shop classroom. He could practically taste the metallic iron of blood in the air.

Behind him came the hollow clomping sounds of the three Mindless men as they followed him up the ramp. Max felt around and ran straight forward into the ship's inner darkness, triggering an automatic light that blinded the room with a white hot brightness. Max instinctively lifted his left arm over his head to shield his eyes and squinted into the brightness.

He was in a long curving hallway, not unlike one that could be found in a science fiction movie. The walls were the same hollowed metal as the ramp and, as he squinted into the light, a steam began to emit from vents at the top of the corridor just above him with a faint hissing sound.

He had to move.

Max continued to run along the corridor at a much slower pace. The groans and moans of the Mindless behind him began to echo through the enclosed hollowed area and he knew that he had to get behind the Mindless for his plan to work.

Max rounded the corridor and saw that the metallic wall veered out slightly into what seemed like a hatched doorway. It was still wide open and as he made his way past the doorway he noticed that part of the walls along this corridor changed to become a fish tank-like casing with green jelly-like water bubbling away inside it. No matter, he now had a place to hide.

Max squeezed himself behind the inner side of the doorway's hatch and waited. His right hand with the Visitors' gun was raised in front of him ready to strike and Max pulled his favourite knife from the sheath in his boot. He took a deep breath to steady himself after his run and held it in.

As he waited silently behind the doorframe he could hear the groans and the echoing footsteps of the Mindless come closer. Suddenly they burst through the opening of the doorway, one after the other, with the spikey-haired blonde leading the charge. The black-haired Mindless followed and the Middle Eastern Mindless Max had freed from the tree came trudging up last, dropping blood and pieces of flesh from the hole in its chest along the floor.

The three Mindless moved past Max in their single-minded mission to find him, but he stayed silently waiting for them to move ahead. Their groans echoing off the walls were all he could hear until a sudden wailing sound began to emanate from the outside of the ship. Max covered his ears and the blinding white light that filled his eyes began to bleed into a bright red colour.

He could feel the ship underneath him begin to hum and vibrate with energy and Max knew that the Visitors were getting ready to cut their losses and leave. He needed to find Victoria and get out now.

With no time to waste, Max removed his hands from his ears and took in the offensive wailing sounds. He peaked out from behind the corridor and could now hear a mix of shrieks and rumbles and wet slick sounds in front of him.

The Mindless had found the Visitors and had begun their attack.

It was time to find Victoria.

CHAPTER 12

Victoria's vision was filled with nothing but a blinding white light and all her body could feel was a pain so fierce she was practically numb. The pain was emanating from inside her — specifically inside her womb from her unborn baby — but she was completely frozen to the point where she couldn't feel her fingers or her toes let alone move them organically

She was trapped in a blinding bubble of white light and pain inside herself.

Suddenly her vision began to swim and the pain inside her began to ebb and flow like the ocean. It reverberated off her but began to ease, and Victoria could suddenly feel her fingers and toes again as she twitched them. Slowly, the feeling in her body began to come back, the pain in her womb subsided and her vision began to restore.

Victoria blinked several times to free her mind of the white light, but it was still blindingly light wherever she looked. Her eyes adjusted slowly and she looked around, finding herself standing in a room completely made of white and being unable to determine where she was or even what direction she was standing in. There were no corners and no edges from what she could see, and she could barely register that she was standing up because the floor was eerily similar. If she couldn't feel the hardness of floor underneath her, she would have considered herself floating in this strange white light.

Her bleary eyes zoned in on the only other large hunk of mass in the room. It wasn't the Captain that had compelled her behind the hedges – it was the Commander, strong and mummified looking like the others but its stance on its hind legs was straighter, giving it the air of authority. It closed the space between them easily on its thick hind legs and its elongated cranium lifted towards her. Victoria could see its beady nostrils flair quickly as it sniffed before a bright blue ring flashed from where its iris would be in its dark eyes.

Victoria reeled backwards at the sight. She had looked at countless Visitors, Mindless Visitors, Mindless, and humans in the eyes, but something about this particular Visitor felt different.

Victoria could feel nothing but dread leaden her stomach.

Despite being compelled to look into its eyes, Victoria wrenched her eyes away and saw her chainsaw lying on the ground. It was rusted and covered in congealed purple blood, but Victoria looked at it like it was an old friend and a rush of emotion came bursting through her heart.

Victoria quickly took stock of herself as the last of her trance began to fade. Her mind pulsed black at the edges as she realised the metallic Visitors' cuff that she wore on her wrist had been removed. She reached for her gun holsters at her thighs to find them empty, and she could feel the knife she had stowed in her boot had also been confiscated.

She was weapon-less in a white room with nothing in it but herself, the Commander of the Visitors from another planet, and her aged chainsaw. She had to admit it all seemed rather hopeless.

Victoria turned strongly and deliberately back to the Commander and looked it dead in its hollow blue-rimmed eyes, deciding to do the only thing she could do – talk.

"Who are you?" she demanded of it, "Why do you have my chainsaw? Why are you here?" she practically screamed, not expecting an answer.

The Commander opened its beak like mouth and let out a shrill sound that pierced Victoria's ears, but surprisingly a deep voice flowed through her mind in a broken fashion, the words chopped with silence as it paused to find the right words.

"I am the Commander," the voice in her head said, "and you are on my ship. This world belongs to us and we have come to claim it."

Victoria was stunned. She stared at the Commander in front of her.

"Is this real? Can I really hear you?" she asked it, aghast at what was happening. Again the Commander opened its beak-like mouth and emitted a series of shrieks and clicks, but as the same deep voice flowed through her head, its physical sounds deafened in her ears.

"Yes but this is highly unusual – we do not usually converse with lower lifeforms," it answered and Victoria balked at the idea of being considered a lower lifeform. After what they had done to rid the world of the first settlement of Visitors that had invaded the planet, they were in no way inferior. This Commander knew that yet still toyed with her like she was an ant.

The Commander continued, "We have identified from this weapon you lodged in one of our own that you carry the DNA of our kind and I believe that this is why I am able to communicate with you."

"What do you mean the DNA of your kind?" Victoria demanded, extremely fearful for the quiet foetus inside her. Her mind flooded with ideas and stories of experiments and alien kidnappings that had plagued conspiracy theorists back when the world was whole. But the fear subsided somewhat – she could remember the day her child was conceived and there was absolutely no way that any of the Visitors had been involved or abducted her. They hadn't even landed on Earth at that point!

No way was this possible.

"You were compelled by one of our kind during the first settlement, were you not?" the Commander asked. "When this occurred, your foetus was imprinted on while it was developing its DNA. It was altered slightly in your womb."

Victoria thought back to the Visitors' first arrival and how the Visitor had stunned and compelled her when she had attacked it to protect Ian Peters. She had been pregnant then, but she hadn't known it.

If she had known at the time, she may have acted differently.

"You're saying that when I was taken that first time, that Visitor left some of its DNA imprinted on my child?" Victoria asked, shocked. Her hands instinctively clutched protectively at her stomach. She couldn't believe this – Jacinta had been right.

"Yes. Not much – a strand or two. But it makes your child important; one of us. It is a hybrid and we did not anticipate this. It needs to be studied," he Commander told her.

Victoria felt a surge of fear travel up from the pit of stomach. This otherworldly Visitor wanted to study her unborn child like a lab rat.

Suddenly the fear in her stomach hardened like lead and Victoria felt a rush of anger instead. Who was this 'Commander' to dictate what would happen to the child that belonged to her and Max?

"I will never let you study my child," Victoria told the Commander through clenched teeth, the anger rising within her. "You say it has a strand or two of your DNA? Well the rest is made up of human DNA – mine and its father's. Just because it shares some of your DNA does not mean it is yours to do what you want with it!" Her voice was rising now.

"You and everything on this world belongs to us. You think your Gods made you? They abandoned you. This world is just another planet in the galaxy, unprotected and unnecessary." The Commander's deep voice in Victoria's head flowed with a flash of irritancy and anger now.

"We are superior in every way and we take what we want. We know how your world works, how you pathetic humans live and breathe," the Commander continued. "We have conducted countless studies on your kind, perfecting the virus that you call the Mindless, studying your world to ensure we would be triumphant when we arrived to claim it. The damage you have done to the first settlement and to my fleet does not spare you from our intentions. But with this child you do bring complications. You alone will be spared as we do intend to study you, to experiment on the imprint and the DNA, for you to have the child and for us to acquire knowledge on this hybrid afterwards."

"Over my dead body," Victoria's anger flared.

"That will be arranged once the child is born," the Commander answered with finality.

Victoria stiffened as the idea of her future flashed before her eyes – stuck in this white room, being compelled and imprinted on and studied constantly; giving birth to her child and watching it be taken away before her own life ended. Her life would be nothing but pain and misery, like a milking cow whose calf is torn from her for being born male, and primarily useless for the milking industry. Her unborn child would be poked and prodded, and if it wasn't killed it would be raised with these strange Visitors, used and tortured at their hands.

Victoria had killed countless Mindless in a decayed and infested world, battled mysterious Visitors from another planet, and ripped apart friendships in order to secure her unborn baby's survival.

She had come too far and worked too hard to allow this Commander to take it all away from her now.

Victoria thought quickly, unaware as to whether the Commander could read her actions and intentions before they took place. She quickly made for her trusty chainsaw lying on the white floor beneath her to the Commander's side, but the Commander used its strong hind legs to jump at her, knocking her off her feet and skidding away from her weapon.

"You cannot stop this from happening," the Commander's voice decreed as it crouched over her, pining her down with its strong legs and holding her in place. It dipped lower and she saw its blue rimmed irises flash inside the dark pits of its eyes and she turned her head away in defence to avoid being compelled again.

Lying next to her was the chainsaw, the blades rusted and congealed. It may not even turn on, but it was something. Victoria flung her arm out and strained to reach the weapon, her fingers grasping at nothing as she stretched and reached.

It was no good, the chainsaw was too far away.

The weight of the Commander was heavy on top of her, but she noted that it had pinned her legs and was avoiding pressing its weight on her stomach. It was keeping clear of her womb and the unborn baby, meaning she had a small window of opportunity.

Victoria turned back to face the Commander and quickly bucked, straining against the heavy mass of muscles and contorted skin. The Commander was heavy against her, but it moved slightly to ensure the space between it and her womb was still available. Victoria used its unease for her unborn child to her advantage and bucked her hips again, creating enough space for her to push her hip out to one side and slide out from under the Commander.

With the creation of this small new space, Victoria continued to swing her hips from side to side, using her hands to push at the strong mass of Commander above her to slide out from under it. Confused by the slippery technique, the Commander lost its footing as Victoria slid her ankle bone under it and kicked, pushing the Commander into a roll off of her.

Finally free and moving quickly, Victoria scrambled to her feet and keeping low, covered the distance between her and the chainsaw. She heard the Commander let out a loud and angry shriek behind her as she grabbed the machine and pulled the chain.

Nothing happened.

"Come on, come on, come on, *come on!*" Victoria chanted as she pulled the cord again and again, trying to roar the rusted chainsaw into life. The Commander was back on its feet now and moving towards her defiantly. It knew it was going to win.

Victoria stopped pulling and breathed in deeply, closing her eyes momentarily. This was her weapon and an extension of her that she knew like the back of her hand. It had never let her down.

With one last hard pull of the chain, Victoria felt the rip and whir of the rusted blades coming back to life. She opened her eyes quickly and saw some congealed blood splatter slightly on the white floor as it cleared.

Victoria knew there wasn't much fuel left in it to keep the chainsaw going. She had to act now.

Victoria jumped forward and closed the distance between her and the Commander who was still moving towards her. She swung the chainsaw and ripped the rusted blades straight through its arm. The Commander screamed in agony as its grey mottled arm fell to the floor and purple liquid oozed out of the ragged hole the chainsaw had left behind. Without stopping, Victoria moved her chainsaw to the next arm, the mucus membrane already shimmering on the arm she had just lopped off.

The sight could have almost been hilarious – this grey almost-mummified creature in front of her staggering around screaming, its arms lying twitching on the floor. But Victoria had no time for hilarity. She pulled the chainsaw up over her head and swung it down like an axe straight into the Commander's cranium.

The Commander continued to let out a series of high pitched screams as the rusty blades drew their way through its skin and bone of its cranium. It fell to its knees as green brain matter and purple blood sprayed out from under the chainsaws blades and covered Victoria head to toe. Victoria let out a deafening roar as she continued to hack the chainsaw into the screaming Commander, its blue irises flashing like a torch running out of battery.

The Commander let out an ear-piercing shriek before a loud groan. There was a loud pop and suddenly the chainsaw sputtered out with its blades still deep inside the Commander's cranium. Newly reunited, Victoria had used her favourite weapon to slice the Commander straight down through its head.

With no chance of further use from the chainsaw, Victoria let go of her weapon and the Commander's thick mass fell backwards onto the floor into a pool of its own purplish blood and green brain matter. The membrane that had covered its arms had slowed and thinned, but Victoria noted that the clear liquid had begun to form around the chainsaw that was lodged deep into its face and head.

It would take a while, but the Commander would heal eventually. Victoria had to get out of there before that happened.

Victoria leant down and grabbed one of the Commander's severed arms which still flailed around uselessly in a pool of its own blood. The arm she was holding had the Commander's cuff on it and she used the series of buttons she had learnt all that time ago to free the cuff from its wrist. It clambered to the floor and Victoria dropped the arm again, instead picking up the cuff. She fastened it to her own wrist and started taking in the other controls that must be on the cuff. There had to be a button that released her from whatever white Hell she was stuck in.

Suddenly a whooshing sound came from behind her and Victoria felt a gust of wind that rustled her hair. She turned, placing her arm to her eyes to shield her from the sudden change in light that filled the room.

That was easy – she hadn't even pressed any buttons yet.

"Victoria!" came a distinct voice. It was Max!

"Max!" Victoria answered as she rushed forward, meeting her husband in a tight embrace halfway to the door. She breathed in his familiar scent, amazed at her good fortune.

"I thought I had lost you forever!" Max told her, pulling away to take her in. She was aware that she was covered completely in the blood of the Visitor and she wiped her face with the back of her sleeve, smearing the blood even further. Max leaned up and wiped her face with the back of his own sleeve, clearing a bit away for her.

"I thought you did too," Victoria said softly and Max pulled her in for a long hard kiss, blood or no blood. He held her face in his hands and she felt so good to have his lips pressed against her own. Between them, Victoria felt a swift movement in her belly and realised that her baby was responding to the electricity of their kiss.

Victoria pulled away and looked down breathlessly, clutching her stomach.

"Is everything OK with the baby?" Max asked, concerned. He placed one of his large hands over her belly and when the baby kicked his eyes met hers in amazement. It was the first time he had felt it move.

"Everything is fine," Victoria answered, smiling. She'd tell Max what the Commander had said about the Visitor DNA later. All she wanted to do right now was to enjoy the moment of being together again as a family – and being alive.

The moment was cut short with a series of groans and shrieks coming from the doorway behind them. Max and Victoria pulled away from each other and took in the Mindless that was hurtling towards them through the door. It was the black-haired Mindless; it looked a lot worse with its clothing and its face completely covered in purple blood and it stumbled in with strands of bloody muscle being dragged behind from its ripped calf.

The Mindless ran towards them and Victoria and Max parted like the Red Sea as the Mindless man ran straight through them and stumbled, landing on its knees in front of the body of the Commander. The shiny mucus was zipping the contents of the Commander's skull back together slowly, the chainsaw being pushed slowly out of its head.

The Commander was still alive and the Mindless could still detect the heartbeat. The black-haired Mindless grabbed the Commander and began tearing into the flesh of its abdomen, using his strong arm muscles to rip through the hardened skin of the creature.

"Do you still have the remote for the bombs?" Max asked Victoria, turning towards her. Victoria started patting her pockets down, looking for the remote control that she had had in her pockets and praying that the Visitors hadn't removed it when they had taken her other weapons. She sighed in relief as she pulled out the small black remote control garage door opener that Professor Malone had rigged to ignite the bombs and held it up for Max to see.

"Good, let's get out of this ship and blow it! That will take care of the Mindless Visitors that are being turned," Max answered as he grabbed Victoria's hand and led her to the exit of the white room. As they began to run Victoria slipped the remote control back into the pocket of her pants for safe keeping.

Coming out into the hallway Victoria took in the ship. Her memory of walking through the hallways had been drenched in brilliant white light so she hadn't really taken in what it had meant to be inside a Visitors' spaceship.

The hallway was long, curving and metallic and was drenched in a white light. A steam was being emitted from vents that lined the roof of the hallway and along several panels of the hallway walls was something that looked like a fish tank, only containing green bubbling jelly instead. Echoing down the metallic hallway, high pitched shrieks of the Visitors could be heard at a piercing level. There were several groans and moans that Victoria knew to be the Mindless, and it was then that she noted several pools of purple blood on the floor.

"Come on, this way!" Max said as he led Victoria left down the corridor, away from the echoes of screams and groans, their feet thumping hollowly along the metallic floor below her. They ran past a body of a Mindless with blonde spikey hair lying crumped against the luminous wall, its spine broken but its arms and gaping mouth still reaching for them. Purple and dark red blood was splattered and dripping in pools along the hallway and Victoria knew this Visitors' ship would be crawling with Mindless Visitors by now.

Max and Victoria ran through an opened hatched doorway that jutted out slightly from the corridor and she could make out a bright light and the exit ramp in front of her. They were almost there!

Thudding down the hollowed ramp Victoria blinked against the darkened rusty colour of the world around her. Her senses were in overload as she squinted into the sky and saw clouds of black smoke emanating from the hills far away from the city. The air had changed from being the stale metallic cold of the ship into a warm and dusty quality that threatened to suffocate her.

"Has the rest blown?" Victoria asked Max as he continued to hold her hand and run with her down the ramp and back up the hill to where she had crouched behind the hedge. Her legs burned with adrenaline at the change of terrain.

"I hope so," Max answered as they reached the top of the hill. They kept running behind the office building before Victoria realised they were a safe distance away and slowed to a stop, letting go of Max's hand and causing him to slide to a stop in front of her.

"Then let's end this," Victoria said and pulled the garage door opener out of the pocket of her pants. She held the control up for him to see and Max nodded in agreement.

"You messed with the wrong world," Victoria sneered as she pressed the button of the remote control. Max and Victoria waited with baited breath for the explosion to confirm that the bomb had worked. It took a minute, but suddenly the air was filled with an explosion that rocked the ground beneath them. A huge ball of fire expanded over the tops of the building and took hold of the Visitors' ship that they had just been inside.

They had done it. They had destroyed the ship and they were alive!

Max and Victoria turned to each other and wrapped themselves in each other's arms; bloodied, sweating, and out of breath.

The war was finally over.

EPILOGUE

The war against the Visitors may have finally been over, but the battle for survival against the Mindless still raged.

The activity from the numerous fires of the Visitors' ship drew all the Mindless in the area towards the flames, looking for their next feast. Each group had been charged to take care of the ships that they had each bombed, so they dutifully watched the fires burn themselves out and ensured removal of any spot fires that threatened to rip through the forests around the smouldering hunks of metal.

It was long tiresome work, picking off Mindless that wandered towards the flames and watching the fire burn itself out, but they didn't mind. Victoria found the fire comforting, delighting in the fact that the world was once again safe from Visitors from another planet.

But as the teams of two each worked at burning the bodies of the dead, controlling the fires of the ship and taking down any wandering Mindless that came across the flames, they were unaware that they too were being watched.

High on the roof of the old apartment building where the group had once lived, a tall and beautiful dark-skinned woman regarded the couple through the sights of her rifle. She had the gun aimed directly at the brunette head of Victoria as she busied herself lifting a rotting corpse onto a pile of bodies that acted as a funeral pyre that she and Max had roughly put together.

If the dark-skinned woman squeezed the trigger, Victoria's life would be over. Her head would explode with the impact of the bullet and she would fall right into the pile of dead she was conveniently making. The idea was tempting. After all, Victoria Stone had been the one to ruin Jacinta Reinhart's life.

When Victoria had announced she was pregnant, it had been after the first settlement of Visitors had attacked. The announcement of her pregnancy had come as a shock, but her demands for Jacinta to leave the group and travel in the opposite direction from the group was like putting a gun to her temple and pulling the trigger herself. It was dangerous to go off on your own, and Victoria knew the chance of lone survival was slim.

But the chance was not as slim as having a child.

Jacinta Reinhart was a strong woman and she overcame obstacles easily. While she had told the group she would go in the opposite direction, Jacinta had grown so angry and bitter that she had wanted revenge. How dare they put her at risk like that? How dare they throw her out into the cold by herself after all she had done for them?

So Jacinta had followed them. She had lost the group at times, and it turns out she had actually moved ahead of them. As she raided a nearby convenience store for basic supplies it had been there that she had run into Blake Mirchoff, a tall and attractive man with spikey blonde hair and a five o'clock shadow.

Jacinta had actually saved Blake in a rare moment of humanity when the convenience store had been overrun by the

177

Mindless, and he had been very grateful for her help. She was glad she had decided to turn back and help him because he told her about a community that had been surviving against the Mindless invasion that were holed up in a country club outside the remnants of the city.

Happy to be finally welcomed for once, Blake brought Jacinta back to his community, who had been ecstatic to find a strong and capable woman who knew what they were up against. Jacinta had quickly made herself at home in the community, hunting and providing watch against attacks of the Mindless, which had been greatly appreciated by the small new group.

Jacinta had finally felt like she was home when she saw the unmistakable arrival of the Visitors. There were more than last time and she knew this was a bad sign, but when she and Blake went on a scouting missing and Jacinta had seen her old group she knew that they were acting on it. Upon her welcome advice, her new community hung back while Victoria and Max cleaned up the mess that they had no doubt made in their destruction of the first settlement.

And cleaning up the mess they were. Jacinta could feel her finger around the trigger itch to end the life of this unconscionable woman, but a sound of heavy footsteps pulled her from target practice and Jacinta whipped around.

Standing at the edge of the roof near the exit stairwell was Ian Peters. He was looking much better than he had been when Jacinta had found him lying on the sidewalk near the old apartment building. He had been near death, completely ripped open and torn limb from limb, but as she had stumbled across him Jacinta found a faint clear membrane covering his wounds.

His connection to the Visitors meant that he had developed their regenerative abilities. Ian Peters, patient zero from the Mindless infection, had been healing himself from the attack that had left him lifeless and exposed on that road for days.

Jacinta had waited with him for some time while he healed, protecting him, and when he was finally whole again she moved him back to the apartment where she had waited for his wounds to fully heal. It took several days, but by the time Ian Peters was conscious and talking, Jacinta had told him the whole story – how Victoria and Max Stone had abandoned them and left them behind in an attempt to save themselves and their baby.

Ian had been just as furious as Jacinta had been at the thought of being abandoned and agreed to accompany her in her journey for revenge against the Stones. He joined her in following their trail and had been with Jacinta at the convenience store when they rescued Blake, also being integrated into the new community with ease. Jacinta had been surprised at how the nervous man she had once known had completely changed.

Ian Peters was no longer nervous, but a steady and collected person. He spoke with intelligence and acted with integrity. The bites that covered his body had healed thanks to his Visitor physiology and to Jacinta's nursing skills, and he tucked them away behind a smart light blue collared shirt and full length jeans, refusing to speak a word of his involvement in the end of the world.

It was this Ian Peters who stood behind Jacinta now, taking in the sight of his friend on the apartment's rooftop.

"How are they going?" he asked Jacinta as he walked up to stand next to her. Jacinta turned back to face the road below.

"They're cleaning up at the moment. They should be conked out pretty soon I think," Jacinta answered, setting her sights through the scope of her gun again. Ian put a steady hand on Jacinta's shoulder and she lowered the gun in response.

"It won't be long now," Ian told her and Jacinta smiled widely, answering him.

"Soon we can have our revenge."

READ WHAT HAPPENS NEXT IN

Cosmic Decay: Absolution

Coming Soon

PROLOGUE

Revenge can be a powerful weapon when wielded by slighted egos and hardened minds. When the world was filled to the brim with people and possessions, it seemed that any wrongdoing could be punished as severely as one desired. Justice would try to prevail but routinely failed, and matters were taken into blood-covered hands.

Eventually, wielding blood-covered hands was all that was possible, as the world slowly decayed at the vicious touch of others. Many proclaimed that the violent and destructive force of the hidden atrocities of human nature had been the world's downfall, but the few survivors left knew differently.

The world had crumbled into disarray in a short five and a half year time period, as Earth's population fell victim to a deadly rage-fuelled virus that transformed humans into the Mindless – hungry and angry pillars of the dead who roamed the world looking for fresh blood and beating hearts. Their minds and bodies decayed rapidly under the elements of nature, which rose up to claim what the humans had left behind, but their bloodthirsty violence cemented the true nature of the human race.

The Mindless roamed these desolate streets of the world's cities and towns, searching to quench the bloodlust that never ceased, but chose to lay dormant until activity pulled them towards food. Animals were few and far between, taken down by the Mindless and surviving humans in search of living flesh.

But the surviving humans were even scarcer.

Small pockets of those who were strong enough to carry on, rose up amongst the hordes of hungry Mindless, struggling to preserve the human race from extinction. These survivors had soon become privy to the real race to seek control of Earth, not just the ravenous and decaying Mindless but from Visitors from another world.

It became uncovered that these Mindless creatures were the product of a virus that had been leaked into the human race by patient zero – a nervous man named Ian Peters who had found himself in a classic "alien abduction" conspiracy one night long before the world had decayed.

The contamination that Ian Peters unleashed onto the world was an accident, but one that was destined to occur. The virus spread quickly, seeking and destroying the human brain until only the hypothalamus area functioned – the part of the brain where aggression, hunger and violence became the only possible compulsion.

The Visitors from another world had studied Ian Peters and others like him, developing this virus specifically to destroy the Earth's population and making them unable to fight back against a settlement from the Visitors who wished to seek ownership of the Earth, for it was an important resource that would be beneficial to the Visitors and to free it from the bloody hands of the human race seemed like the best possible solution.

But others living on the Earth were not so welcoming and accepting of this plan. Some resourceful humans had survived the contamination and had fought back against the initial settlement.

The Visitors had spent years planning and arranging the tools and planting the virus amongst the humans that inhabited the planet, and had agreed that the first settlers would approach the world and systematically remove the contamination – both the virus and the leftover human inhabitants. They would then take their claim of the world and continue their dominion of this new realm.

But the Visitors were surprised when the primitive minds of the surviving humans laid the Visitors plans to waste – seeing the first settlers failing in their cleansing of the contamination of Earth.

The early settlers had not intended that the humans would have survived against their sophisticated and deadly bio-weapons, and had come unprepared for a fight. Distracted under their inflated egos, the Visitors had lost the battle for ownership of the Earth.

But they would not lose the war.

Across the gulf of space, a fleet of ships filled with Visitors awaited a signal from the first settlers, indicating the success of their mission and the start of a new life on Earth. But the beeping pulse it received was actually the signal of a different meaning – a distress signal.

The settlement had failed.

In anger and revenge, and in a last attempt to reclaim what the Visitors saw as rightfully theirs, the fleet charged ahead in the course for Earth. Their ships landed throughout the original settlers areas within the city and searched the remains of their brethren under the watchful eye of the Commander. The Commander sent its best Captain in search of the person behind the attack – a woman who smelt of humanity, of caked dirt, a tang of metal, and a fierce smell that belonged to the Visitors own blood. She was strong and determined, and the smell of their own kind had been too overwhelming to ignore.

The Captain and the Commander searched for this human, but didn't need to scour the Earth as they thought they would have. The woman came to them with a group of other survivors, an army of the Visitor's very own Mindless creatures, and was wielding their very own weapons at them – a metallic cuff that contained their protection and their information.

But that wasn't all. The humans had moulded their technology into an advanced weapon, creating an explosive device that had been secretly planted under each of the Visitor's ships and detonated, destroying the ships they had brought with them across the galaxy and turning their army of Visitors into armies plagued with the Mindless virus. Under the virus, the Visitors were unable to heal like they usually would be able to, and in that the humans seemed to understand.

They attacked mercilessly until every Visitor and ship had been destroyed.

All except the Captain. The Captain had been sent on its scouting mission to uncover the human woman and bring her back to the Commander. He discovered she was pregnant and had a few strands of the Visitor's DNA within the foetus of her child, something that had occurred when she had been compelled under the Visitor's spell while her child had been growing, unbeknownst to her, inside her womb.

The Captain had completed his mission, and had brought the woman to the prison cells of the Commander's ship. As the Commander had taken over her interrogation within the cell, The Commander had sent the Captain back out onto the battlefield.

The Captain had made for cover of a row of houses up the road, trying desperately to seek contact with its brethren but was unable to reach the appropriate levels of communication. The Captain sensed the tearing sensation of its fellow Visitors and stopped in its tracks.

Around it, it could sense the explosions of the ships they had all arrived in – the gas leaking and tearing the atoms apart in the heat. Its fellow brethren were shrieking in terror, and those that had been turned into Mindless were overcome with hunger before there was nothing but silence.

The Captain could hear them all – their pain, their suffering, and their destruction. It was almost too much to bare.

Behind it, the explosion of the Captain's very own ship rocked the Captain to its core. It had been the Captain of that ship for years and to lose it was to have one of its own arms be cut off and never reattached in its healing manner. It turned back towards the ship and raced through the trees.

As it reached the edge of the tree line, the Captain saw smouldering trees and blackened earth take over. It stopped and crept forward, taking in the destruction before it. Its beloved ship was nothing burning metal raining from the sky, with the trees and ground around it completely decimated under the otherworldly gas. Blasts of fire were everywhere as ash filled the stale air.

It was then that the Captain saw them – the human woman and her mate moving slowly to their feet near a building that was up the hill and away from the Captain's ship. They were wrapped in each other's arms, kissing, celebrating their victory.

The Captain searched its vast mind and found nothing. It could no longer hear the screams and shrieks of its brethren, or feel the hunger of the Mindless Visitors. They were nowhere to be found on this Earth that they had come to claim.

The Visitors from another world were dead.

The Captain almost let out a shrill shriek of pain and torment, but kept its rage inside. Its whole body shook where it stood, it's rippling muscles under its tight mottled skin felt like it was going to spring free under the pressure. It knew that it couldn't make a sound because the humans would find it and destroy it like they had done to all his others.

Stranded on this alien world without a ship, without a crew or anything in its species, and at the mercy of the humans the Captain weighed up its options. It could let the humans find it and kill it like they had done to its brethren, but the Captain knew that it didn't want to die.

It had come too far and done too much to roll over and let the humans win now.

The Captain continued to weigh up the options. It could survive and use the leftover materials to try and build another ship and get back to its home world, but with the leak of the otherworldly gas a safe return seemed unlikely.

So the only real outcome was to stay and seek its revenge on the humans that did this.

The Captain knew that this was the best option, and with the woman carrying a child that had the DNA of its own kind staying on this God forsaken earth was the only way that he would be able to ensure the survival of its own race.

Everything was backwards now, and the power had shifted out of the Visitor's hands.

But was it ever really in their hands?

The Captain was certain that it should be. They had the power to create the world that the humans now lived in and they should have the power to take it all away from them. The Commander had been forthcoming in the fact that the unborn child was paramount to the Visitors, and the Captain was loyal until the end.

It had to bide it's time and wait. There was nothing the Captain could do while it was growing inside the womb of the woman. She was too well-protected, and any damage to her would result in the death of the child and the Captain's plans for revenge.

The Captain's body stopped shaking with rage. It now finally had a plan.

The Captain and the child could still claim this world as their own. It would be the end of the humans forever.

All it had to do was wait.

Acknowledgements

Charlotte Johnson, Nicole Powell, Sophie Carberry and Tabitha Cole – Without your unending support and love through my darkest of times, I never would have made it through to be publishing my second novel. You are the most amazing, strong, powerful women in the world and I appreciate all of your love.

Colin and Alison Lewis – Thank you for all of your love and support throughout not only my entire writing career, but for my entire life. I love that writing runs through our veins.

Byron Carr – Thank you so much for designing me yet another amazing book cover and promotional material. Your design services are outstanding, and you will always be my Max Stone.

Marion Mapham – Thank you once again for your editing services, putting this world together for me and making sure it makes sense.

Thank you to all my friends and family for their unwavering support and unconditional love and advice. I couldn't do any of this without you.

And for all the ghosts that left me behind, I hope you enjoyed the world I put you in.

About the Author

Courtney Hope is an author from Canberra, Australia, writing for many different publications and blogs including her own event planning blog The Party Connection, and a horror pop culture blog called This Side of Sanguine.

She may look like a cupcake, but Courtney is wickedly dark, enjoying listening to rock music, drinking too much red wine, watching too many horror movies, and living an environmentally-friendly hygge lifestyle. She is a vegan, a dog owner, and a pop culture fan.

She had written a party planning handbook called *Secrets of a Party Planner,* as well as *Cosmic Decay: Contamination.* Her third novel in the series, *Cosmic Decay: Absolution* will be available in the future.

www.courtneyhope.com.au
www.thepartyconnectionaustralia.com
www.thissideofsanguine.com

www.ingramcontent.com/pod-product-compliance
Lightning Source LLC
Chambersburg PA
CBHW071435100726
47908CB00004B/1159